A MATTER OF DAYS

A MATTER OF DAYS

Stories by ALBERT LEBOWITZ

Louisiana State University Press
Baton Rouge and London   1989

Copyright © 1961, 1963, 1971, 1989 by Albert Lebowitz
All rights reserved
Manufactured in the United States of America

98 97 96 95 94 93 92 91 90 89   5 4 3 2 1

Designer: Laura Roubique Gleason
Typeface: Caledonia
Typesetter: The Composing Room of Michigan, Inc.
Printer: Thomson-Shore, Inc.
Binder: John H. Dekker & Sons, Inc.

Library of Congress Cataloging-in-Publication Data
Lebowitz, Albert, 1922–
  A matter of days : stories / by Albert Lebowitz.
    p.   cm.
  ISBN 0-8071-1417-0 (alk. paper)
  I. Title.
PS3562.E27M38   1989
813'.54—dc19   88-22054
                                                      CIP

Many of the stories herein first appeared, in slightly different form, in the following publications: *Contact, Mutiny, Perspective,* and *Quixote.* "Fun and Game Days," copyright © 1963 by Albert Lebowitz, originally appeared in *Stories for the Sixties,* edited by Richard Yates, published by Bantam Books, Inc.

The paper in this book meets the guidelines for permanence and durability of the Committee on Production Guidelines for Book Longevity of the Council on Library Resources. ∞

For those who have made my days:
Nay, Joel, Judith, Sophie and Prousty

CONTENTS

I. MOTHER'S DAY   1

II. DAY LABOUR   8

III. HIS DAYS ARE AS GRASS   20

IV. DEAR DAYS   32

V. DAYS WHEN BIRDS COME BACK   52

VI. FUN AND GAME DAYS   69

VII. A DAY IN THE LIFE OF A DOG   87

VIII. THE DAY OF TRIALS   100

IX. A DAY IN THE LIFE OF GOD   110

A MATTER OF DAYS

I

MOTHER'S DAY

She had no pretensions. Her nose was slightly humped and she was tall, thin, muscular. Her voice was a croak and her blonde hair was limp. Phyllis Stein stood on the bed and recited: give me a home where the buffalo roam and the deer and the antelope play. She fell back on the bed and startled her dachshund, Uriah, into a bark. He looked at her from David's pillow until, as dogs do (one of their strengths), he refused to play chicken and dropped his eyes. "Sure, while the old man's away, the dog-child will play." At twenty-six Phyllis, knowing, knew she was over the hill.

She fixed on Uriah's unblinking lids. "You are a bad, bad dog." He whined and wagged his whip-handle tail and she heard the scraping in the attic. She shook her fist madly at the ceiling. "You squirrely bastard, I'll get you yet." Uriah bounced off the bed barking his bat-winged head off. She eyed him speculatively, feeling cruel, and of course he looked away, unnerved. An eye for a tooth? Upstairs the harsh digs at the plaster and here forgiveness? "You're a mouth, simply that. Eat our food and show your teeth at night at our lovemaking. Why you and not the squirrel? Come here," she ordered sharply and Uriah, a psychological genius with an infinite capacity for absorbing pain, leaped on the bed and pushed at her face with his black nose. He was a clever one all right. Smart in his genes. Clear concentrate of love. She nuzzled him.

The attic was unfinished. She had never been up there but had David's description. Parallel lines of underpinning and all the insulation exposed and big holes under the eaves where, undoubtedly, empire building was going on. Their entrance was a trapdoor in the ceiling of the second-floor hall. The squirrel's was his own secret. David kept dragging the wooden ladder from the basement and blundering with a flashlight from one board to the next. Phyllis nodded at Uriah. "I am simply no longer amused."

They had tried everything but poison. They were both firm about that: no poison. Everybody but the Humane Society said that poison was the only thing. It was supposed to make the insides bleed and drive animals to water. Finally they would swell out. Phyllis shuddered. The Humane Society said to use a trap but they were eightieth on the waiting list so David went to Central Hardware and all he could get was a wire cage for catching rats alive. It had a compartment for the food and a one-way spring trapdoor. The rat would stand on the door to reach for the food and down he'd go. She couldn't figure out what kind of person would want to catch rats alive. David and she were after lovable game: a squirrel. A damnable, noisy, fun-loving squirrel. So far the trap had been in the attic for three days and not a nibble.

The scraping stopped. Had her voice frightened him? It had frightened Uriah but a window shade rattling could do that. Suppose that it was in the trap? The thought horrified her. This was not part of the game. Urbanites bought traps and baited them and cursed the noises, but one never, never trapped anything. Uriah yapped at invisible sounds (he *saw* sounds) from the street and she shushed him. She held her breath, listening: nothing. She collapsed on her stomach and listened: nothing. Was it trapped? Cowering at the bottom of the cage, wondering what had happened to its fine, new world under the eaves? It *had* to be in the trap. She jerked out of bed and dressed rapidly in shorts and one of David's frayed white shirts. It was exactly noon. She rolled the sleeves up as she went to the basement for the ladder. It was awfully heavy and she had a time getting it up the stairs and almost knocked one of Uriah's eyes out. "Sure," she said to Uriah, "and David's in Jefferson City." She unfolded the ladder under the trapdoor and started up. The trapdoor pushed in easily and she stuck her head inside. The attic was dark and acrid nasty smelling and it was hopeless without a flashlight—and that meant going to the basement again. She stood prayerfully, straining against the darkness, but no, no easy way out, like a good old-fashioned scampering about. And David in Jefferson City. Why did she keep saying that as if it meant anything?

Phyllis went to the basement and found the flashlight in the tool chest. She played the beam around. She wasn't going to be taken in, no sir. It would be just like him not to have batteries and she would be back upstairs and turn it on for nothing. Just like their sex. Uriah was at her heels and she swung around and flashed the beam in his eyes. "You," she challenged. "What are you following me for? Go along and play, you dirty rat. You are, you know." He blinked and whined. "All right," she said. "Come along. But be perfectly quiet, understand? We're taking over this turf." She marched upstairs.

The top of the ladder was not high enough. The only way she could get in was to lift on her hands and she was afraid she'd fall and break her neck. A great loss to the world indeed: Phyllis Stein, graduate student in comparative literature, wife of David, mother of Uriah, boarder of squirrels, today broke her neck while climbing into her attic. They said of her . . . what? Would they mourn? *Should* they? They'd laugh and say, bad joke, Phyl, bad, bad joke. Uriah? Of course. Pure concentrate of love, or had she said that before? She got a knee up and was in the attic. She sat quivering and almost cried. She had forgotten the flashlight and was scared to death of the animal that was waiting. Did squirrels bite? Of course. And with teeth like nutcrackers only sharp. Imagine his terror at being trapped. He would most certainly defend himself and that meant attacking her. Why had she ever thought squirrels were cute? They were almond-eyed inscrutable monsters. She lowered herself through the trapdoor and her legs scrambled at empty air before they found the top of the ladder and she marveled for a moment at David. Was it merely the maleness? He traveled this route over and over without a whimper, even smiling. Of course, that was his thing, smiling. And he hadn't caught the squirrel and that was the main thing.

She started up again with the flashlight and Uriah moaned anxiously at the foot of the ladder. Phyllis laughed breath through her nostrils. "The man of the house, watching his mother's shorts disappearing into darkness and danger. You man you." She poked her head through the opening and flashed the light around until she located the trap. It was at the far end, toward the front near the louvers and she couldn't tell whether the squirrel was trapped or not. She'd have to go in. She placed the flashlight on the floor and pulled herself up. The underpinning boards were about two feet apart and she would have to walk from one to another. Between them she could see the wires and insulation and was convinced that if she missed her footing she would surely poke through the second-floor ceiling.

But the squirrel waited and she had to get on with it. She moved with trembling feet from one board to the other, an unwilling accomplice to the beam of light going first.

The trap was empty. The hoard of almonds lay untouched. She sat on one of the boards with her feet against another and cried with relief and pride. She had climbed the mountain because the squirrel was there and the squirrel wasn't there, so where was he? She did not have long. She became aware of eyes probing her back, testing the softness. What dark corner had he found? Was he under the eaves? Had he learned that she was all of unlearning womankind and that he had planted his flag on her grave? Each animal balanced nature. He scraped behind her, coming closer. She was afraid to turn but kept her light safely on the empty cage and, suddenly, in a gush of terror, urinated. She sat wetting, crying, and in a fit of uncaring turned to face the enemy, sucking him out of the darkness.

It was Uriah, bobbing in and out of sight over the boards, his rear quarters hanging then dropping, his nose surfacing then diving. She watched him in anguish, not believing. The light worried him and he stopped, only a head, body lost between the boards. She tried to explain: You couldn't have and I'll tell you why. The ladder isn't built for you, but that's the least of it. The top of the ladder is easily three feet from the trapdoor and you couldn't have made it unless you were a squirrel. And you are not a squirrel, are you? Are you? "Go away," he said. His wounded eyes gleamed. "I give up. I simply give it up. Now you'll tell me there is no squirrel." She leaned toward the cage and opened the food compartment. The nuts poured on the floor. "You've won," she said to Uriah. "This is for your friend." Phyllis got to her feet and started back across the boards, and as she watched, Uriah turned tail and, bobbing, fled to the trapdoor and dropped, bat-winged ears spread, through the opening. She ran, daring herself to miss the boards and did. Her foot landed hard on the insulation and she felt it give but not enough to cause a break. "You see?" she cried. "I was right. You can go right through the plaster." She slid through the trapdoor and of course Uriah was waiting at the bottom of the ladder, whining and wagging, pretending to have been left behind. The hypocrite but there was no use cross-examining him. Like father, like son. She wouldn't get a word out of him. She went to the bedroom, changed clothes, and sprawled face-upward, listening. She knew that it would begin again. It had to. They were all in on it, laughing at her. And it did, in a demonic, frenzied scampering back and forth that told her plainly: I have friends here. I'm not alone. Who can touch me? Her heart pounded with hate. She would poison him.

Phyllis waited until Uriah was distracted by his invisible noises, then snatched her purse and ran downstairs and out to the car. What was she afraid of? What if Uriah *did* warn him? The squirrel would die.

At the hardware store she had to be careful. Squirrels were bigger, more like pets. They were not to be killed. The ordinances said so. But what was she a lawyer's wife for? Laws defeated laws. He was a trespasser and could be shot at sight. "I want something to poison a rat," she said to the hardware man and he smiled a big, black-gnarled smile. "How many packages?" he asked. "They're one forty-nine each. Can't miss."

"Six," she said shrugging prettily for, after all, she was virginal before the brutal world of extermination, and he whistled softly as he gave her the bag. "That'll kill a lot of rats," he said. She turned and ran before he could imagine what she was up to.

Back at the house, Uriah waylaid her at the front door and leaped for the bag but she kept it away from him, holding it out for him to jump at. "Sure," she coaxed. "It's balls and squeaky mice and dog yummies and dog ambrosia and dog nectar but you can't have any. It's all for your friend upstairs. Run and tell him, why don't you? Go on." He kept jumping, groaning in his eagerness, his wafer-pink tongue lolling to one side and eyes careening. She sat in a living room chair and he kept worrying at the bag. "You fool!" she shouted, exasperated beyond endurance. "Would you die for him too? It's not enough to betray your mother. You must bleed too. Let your guts burst with the pride of blood and for what? A squirrel too big for his britches, who wants the coziest nest on the block." And she wanted, right then and there, in her own brown living room with the walnut tables, to fling the bag down and let Uriah root at will. His fat belly would grind out its misery and he would bash his snout against the toilet bowl and he would swell up like a greedy king and he would pop. And for what? She put the bag on the mantel and cried on Uriah's soft, sausage-skin belly. "Pure concentrate of hate, you're safe," she moaned. "Whatever you do to me, however you turn from me, I'm your mother. You're my life. Without you I'm dead. You see?" And she extracted a package from the bag and held it aloft. "Down my own gullet before." And she saw herself burning, burning toward water, scrabbling on terrible knees to rain-swollen gutters. Lying face downward, clouded by masses of hair. And what would David say to that? Would he, would he have his glass of milk and change into khakis and tee shirt before he lifted her out of the gutter? And the funeral. Who on earth would get the funeral? She wanted to be cremated, yes she did, if only to admit to nothingness once and for all, but would he do it? He wouldn't. Like all lawyers he never threw anything away. She found a pencil and wrote on the package: I, Phyllis Stein, want to make a complete ash of myself. Everything perfectly legal. The letter of the law and perhaps protocol would defer.

"Enough," she said sternly to Uriah. "The law's delay I tell you is everywhere," and she went upstairs to the ladder before she realized that she had left five packages of poison and Uriah downstairs. "It's too much," she said. "Really too much. I'll go mad," and she ran back. If she poisoned her dog, she would surely, instead of the present probably, divorce David, this was the sobering thought she had before she found Uriah tearing at the bag with growls and tugs. She gave him a fierce slap on the rump and gathered up the packages as he bounded away in unbelieving surprise. One just didn't slap, he told her. The packages were toothmarked but unpierced. "You'll live, you dibbuk," she said and went back upstairs. She climbed the ladder and counted her packages at the top—six—and opened the trapdoor. It was unbelievable. She had forgotten the flashlight again. Not that she was nervous, or anything, oh no. She was simply becalmed, hesitating before the final sweep. She began a patient search for the flashlight. It was not on the ladder or on the table near it. She went downstairs and further, to the tool chest in the basement. Nowhere? An omen? That had to be considered. She was in the darkness searching for the light and if she couldn't find it, it meant she should have stayed in bed. What would Odysseus do in the same or similar circumstances? But she was Penelope keeping the house shipshape for her itinerant husband's return, caulking, painting, plastering, shooting trespassers *on sight*. Where on earth was the flashlight? She would prove a point that every good contractor knew: murders should be committed in darkness. She pushed up the ladder and Uriah complained. "You *know*, don't you," she said. "You know exactly where it is. In fact, you've hidden it under some pillow or couch, haven't you? My one, my only, my true son." And when she opened the trapdoor she knew instantly where the flashlight was: ready to her hand, lying on the insulation where it should be. She was able, all was willing, the light, the poison (again she counted the six, stacked in a row on a board) and the desire to kill. She threw the beam carefully around the attic starting from the front and working along the sides. The beam hung, stretched like a death ray in a line to one of the eaves. The squirrel crouched, tail pluming, eyes hard and bright-black, his head frozen in effigy. They looked, she at the squirrel, he at the light. He was gray and, never really having looked at a squirrel before, she noticed that he was mostly fur and that his body was a terribly small tube, not bigger than her vacuum cleaner handle. She looked and knew that she sincerely hated him. He was such a little animal and terribly frightened and just trying to get by. He made his home where he could, and how many nights had he spent spread-eagled on a tree, fur wet and stinking from pelting rain, dreaming of grass and leaves woven into dryness under an anonymous eave (eave, what was that to him?). She picked up her packages one by one and placed them on top of the ladder and shot her beam for one last look. He was gone. All he needed was one chance and he ceased to exist. Had she seen him at all?

With Uriah leaping against her thighs and stomach, Phyllis carried the packages to the bathroom. She opened them thoughtfully and poured the poison into the toilet bowl. At the last she paused and wondered if she dared to lick once, just once, to see what it was like, how much it burned. She didn't dare because it might be habit-forming. She flushed the toilet.

Exhausted, Phyllis flopped on the bed. Uriah leaped up and curled into her body. She lay dry eyed and tense, unable to move or even think. She waited. And then it came, the scraping against the eaves and with it, as though someone had pulled the chain of her thoughts, she began to cry and thrash about the bed. One of her knees caught Uriah sharply in the belly and he leaped away with a yelp of pain.

II

DAY LABOUR

Doth God exact day-labour, light deny'd . . .
—John Milton

On weekday mornings David Stein, who had never learned to live inside himself, would walk his square, fleshy body to the bus stop, a distance of three blocks uphill. The feet, his own, would precede him and make him conscious that the leather of his shoes was cracked and, in places, so worn it wouldn't take polish. From there, while puffing upward, he would realize that his trousers were baggy and his tie spotted. He knew that as a lawyer he should be more presentable but since the body wasn't really his, it didn't seem to matter. He felt, in fact, that he *should* tamper with something that had managed to exist without him for so long.

On the corner he and his would wait for the bus, which would arrive between 8:10 and 8:20 and which, between thirty-five and forty-five minutes later, would unload him downtown. The faces, more familiar than his own because they, belonging to strangers, never changed, had through inevitability, like his own smells or mental processes, become more a part of him than the disturbing visions of his body caught by a camera or a mirror, and he knew instantly which ones would be missing. He never spoke or smiled, nor did they, as if each was afraid to be caught talking to himself, or as if it would be established that they had more in common than the time of day. They were a company of strangers who saw each other every day and who owed each other silence, unlike those on trains who traded fugitive confessions. They knew speechless secrets, the rattling of newspapers, nose pickings, the crack of knuckles, pederastic hips, coughings, spittings. They hated each other, he hated them all, but they endured because they suffered in silence. Except for the blind man.

DAY LABOUR

The blind man got on two stops after David. He was a muscular man with grizzled crew-cut hair, a tilted knob of a nose, and strong chin. His lids, half-closed, vibrated like hovering bees over upturned, milky blue eyes. In cold weather he wore a short coat with a sheepskin collar, and on warm days it would be a sport shirt with loud intersecting checks of blue and gold or red and green. In any weather his trousers would be firmly creased and his shoes, black, would shine ready for barracks inspection.

The blind man, naturally, had a fixed routine, for in his dark world nothing must be out of place. He would be standing on his corner facing toward the curb, his right hand on his black dog's harness, his left arm being held by a plump little slack-jawed woman. When the bus stopped and the door opened, the woman nudged him forward and, his right arm become rigid on the harness, he stepped up briskly behind the dog. Both of them, man and dog, took the two steps casually as though they knew they were performing marvels. The blind man would unclench his fist and drop correct fare into the box, smiling and saying, "Good morning," to the driver. He would then make a quarter turn to the left, almost on his heels, and approach the bench seat directly behind the driver, the one running along the bus's length. If the space was occupied the blind man, standing, would bump knees with the sitting passenger and say, "Would you mind? This is my place." The passenger, confused, would rise and find another seat and others would look quickly away. The dog would receive two surprisingly untender pats from the blind man and would settle on his haunches, front legs braced. Muzzled by a leather strap he would lick his lips as best he could and the blind man would say without inflection, "Good, Corky," and then he would talk, to the driver, to the next passenger, or if they didn't respond, to the world. In any case he would lean forward, chin tilted toward a listener imaginably mounted on a platform above him. "As I see it," he would say, "everything's too soft. That's the trouble with this day and age, too soft. Now take me." He patted his stomach with a blunt-fingered hand so that it thudded with sound. "I do fifty push-ups every morning of my life, yes I do. When's the last time you did fifty push-ups?"

The driver, willing to talk or embarrassed not to (a public servant) would say, "I play handball."

"Okay, that's a nice game, that's all right. That's the game I'd like to take up some day. I can picture that game, a lot more than baseball or football. It takes genuine skill and keeps you in shape. Three wall or four wall?"

"Three wall, in the park."

"Yes sir, that's the ticket. Out in the park in the open air."

His voice was loud and the words distinct and he was the man for the public address system at a sporting event. David would leave his box next to the railing and climb the stone steps, up through the first tier, the second, and finally to the glass enclosed room where the blind man would be huddled over the microphone, talking a blue streak, Corky resting against his policeman's black shoe. David would know he has little time to lose and, with blurring speed, mixing mud and straw, soon has walls erected. The noise, confined, is deafening. David completes the thatched roof and steps back to examine his handiwork. The blind man, Corky, the microphone, are nowhere to be seen but the words, the words, keep pouring out through every crack. It will not do. David labors with bricks, with stones, aluminum siding, prefabricated concrete, stainless steel. It will not do. The words, bell-shaped, shaped like bells, ring out announcing averages, plays, attendance. The inning, the frame, the chukker, the quarter is over but for the blind man there are no periods, he is an eternal sentencer, and David covers his ears with helpless hands.

Or the bird lady would sit next to the blind man and reach down with a coo to pat Corky's low forehead between his black fox ears. The blind man smiled because he loved not the dog but the fuss. "Good dog, Corky," he would say. "Yes," said the bird lady in a breathless trill, "he's such a goodums." And she would busily massage the stolid head while perched excitedly at the edge of the bench, her thin sticks of legs bent in. She had a heavy round body on which she wore, even in cold weather, light gauzy dresses. She had a tiny beak and no chin and watery eyes and was clearly very feminine and unmated.

"Do you have a dog, ma'am?" said the blind man.

"No, I don't," said the bird lady. "They won't let me."

"That's just what I mean, that's what's wrong with this day and age, people just don't have room. They build garages for their cars and don't have room for their pets." Pat, pat, two unfriendly blind man's pats on Corky's head and Corky's fox ears twitched. "A dog, by golly, is still man's best friend, ma'am, did you happen to see the statistics in the Humane Society journal?"

"What? No, I didn't."

"Get this, only one out of fifty burglaries in houses with dogs, yet they won't let you have a dog. You let me talk to them for you, ma'am, and you'd have a dog right enough."

"Goodums," said the bird lady with a final pat. She looked hard at the blind man and pulled a *Reader's Digest* from her shopping bag.

"The way I see it, ma'am," said the blind man, "we're all rushing around from noplace to noplace and don't have time for dogs or anything else. If we'd sit down with our dog in front of a blazing fire, put on our slippers, light our pipe, and read the paper, we'd be a lot better off, believe you me."

The bird lady slapped shut her *Reader's Digest* and dropped it into her shopping bag. "Do you," she chirped, "have a fireplace in your home?"

"Ma'am, I sure don't, but believe me I'd know how to enjoy it if I did. Me and Corky both, wouldn't we, Corky?" Pat, pat.

The bird lady looked at Corky's mouth. "Isn't it a shame you have to put that leather strap around your dog's mouth? He looks as though he wouldn't hurt a flea."

The blind man laughed, a sound that would rattle shades. Passengers shifted dumbly in their seats. "Ma'am, don't let those big brown eyes fool you. Corky knows darned well what to do with his teeth. You know those dogs the police have got trained? I just wish I could spare old Corky, that's all. But don't you worry none, ma'am, he wouldn't lay a hand on you. He knows you're a friend."

David looked at the dog's eyes which were small and round as collar buttons, and David waits at night for the blind man to come home from his evening walk. Corky's muzzle was left at home because it is late and the blind man is going just once around the block. David, banging two frying pans about his head, methodically approaches. The dog, leaping straight in the air, breaks loose and runs and David, banging his pans, circles the blind man who stands motionless, chin on his chest, eyelids twitching, on the sidewalk. When he can no longer stand the frying pans, the blind man walks home alone to sit before the fire and David has bagged himself a blind man.

"Nothing but trouble," repeated the blind man to the shaking man. The shaking man was terribly thin and his body quivered to a terrible tune inside his flesh. Trouser legs flapped around his ankles and his shoulders rotated on ball bearings. He had a preemptive right to the space next to the blind man and when the blind man wasn't there, he proudly took the seat behind the driver. His mouth drooping seemed to sneer but it was only because even his face muscles had gone downhill. The shaking man liked to listen to the blind man. He talked with great pauses, as though his energy bank was met periodically with resistance.

"Did you read . . . where that twelve . . . year old boy . . . got mad . . . and killed . . . his parents . . . with a bread . . . knife?"

"I read about it, yes sir I did," said the blind man. "Did you ever hear of such a crazy thing in all your life? These modern kids, nothing but troublemakers. Why if a son of mine tried pulling a trick like that on me he'd get as good as he gave, believe you me. I'd breadknife him all right. Spare the rod and spoil the child if you ask me. That's still true you know. I'll bet you that crazy kid never got a good old-fashioned licking in all his life. They just let him do whatever he darned well pleased and look what it got them. As good as he gave, that's what he'd get from me."

"The paper . . . said . . . his parents . . . beat him . . . so bad . . . they broke . . . his nose. He . . . stabbed . . . them . . . in their sleep."

"As good as he gave," said the blind man stubbornly. "And I'd sleep with one eye open."

"How many . . . boys . . . you got?"

"Not a danged one. You can have 'em these modern kids. Not in this day and age, not for me, no sir. Not the way they turn out. But I'd sure enough give them what for, you can bet your boots on that."

David is the third man in the ring. The blind man, dressed in black, highly polished trunks, and the blind man, jr., in old-fashioned knickers, circle each other warily, looking for an opening. David senses the lethal power in both fighting men and never takes his eyes off them. The vast arena is hushed, waiting for the explosion.

He who hesitates is lost, says the blind man.

Discretion is the better part of valor, pipes the blind man, jr.

As good as given, says David.

It's better to give than to receive, says the blind man.

Charity begins at home, says jr.

As good as given, says David.

Out of sight, out of mind.

Absence makes the heart grow fonder.

As good as given, says David.

The final bell finds them still flailing away and David leans in to separate them. He declares the match to be a draw and compliments both of them on a clean fight. It isn't, he explains to the crowd, whether you win or lose but how good as you give.

The blind man's voice, David noticed, was without timbre, as though it, too, were blind. It carried effortlessly to every corner of the bus and clung like smoke. It was loud enough to belong to a deaf man and his ears, as though compensatory, were cabbage leaves of greed and when he bent to pat, pat Corky, David saw an original Victor talking machine listening to its dog.

"As I see it," the blind man said to the mumbling man, "they're cowards, nothing but cowards who'd put their tails between their legs and run if you braced them. Just brace them and see how they'd run. Just let one of those hoodlums try me, that's all. I've got something here." He patted his chest over his heart. "I won't tell you what it is but just let them try me. It's a crying shame when you can't walk alone of an evening on a city street."

The mumbling man looked down at his leathery hands, examined his diffident nails, and mumbled.

"What did you say? I couldn't make out what you said, mister," said the blind man in agitation.

The mumbling man mumbled. He was a tall man dressed in neat overalls that spoke for themselves, and he had an eloquent scar etched into his cheek.

"What, what?" yelled the blind man. "Just what is it they want, is what I want to know," said the blind man. "A good day's work for a good day's pay, the sweat of your brow, that's the only way to earn your fig tree I always say. Nothing like sitting down to a nice juicy T-bone paid for by good honest work, believe you me."

The mumbling man sneezed and coughed until his eyes watered.

"I've got something right here," said the blind man. "Someday somebody's gonna get the surprise of his life, won't he, Corky?" Pat, pat. "You'd think people might have learned how to be neighborly, how to get along with their neighbors in all this time, but no sir. They know how to fly to the moon but not how to get along with the guy next door. Why, mister, if the government'd take some of those billions and teach people how to pass the time of day with each other, we'd be a lot better off and that's a fact."

The mumbling man blew his nose and got off the bus, and David waits until the blind man falls asleep at night in his bed. He goes through the clothing carefully hung in the closet, checking each pocket but finds nothing. He tiptoes to the sleeping form, makes sure the blind man is still asleep, places his hand over the blind man's heart and finds nothing. Insinuating his forefinger, the blind man's chest a cabbage ear, David probes for the secret weapon. Patiently, for hours on end, he searches but the weapon is fail-safe hidden and David is plagued with doubts. Perhaps Odysseus has wandered in and is caroling in blind man's tongue, When I say I've something here and you ask what it is, in truth, I may answer, nothing. Nothing is always good for something. David presses a hearing aid against the blind man's chest. Thump, thump. He is comforted by the sound and has the courage to go on. Perhaps he has strayed too far from the eternal big bangs so close to the blind man's heart, like phenomenology or noumena, holism or antinomies. He moves his fingers lightly over the blind man's chest, getting tangled up in curly, manly tufts of hair, failing, but will not admit defeat. He returns to the heart area and sure enough, there clear as day is a Johnson's flesh-colored plaster and in block printed letters the words STIFF UPPER LIP. David looks at the blind man's upper lip and it is true, all truly stiff as a board.

David watched the blind man getting on the bus as usual but this time he stumbled and almost fell over Corky. One of his knees cracked against the dog's ribs and Corky winced in pain. The blind man regained his balance and shrugged off his woman's helping hand. He gave Corky a wallop. He turned his virginal face toward the woman, chin tilted upward, and said something which David could not make out, which he believed to be the only words the blind man ever spoke in his presence he couldn't hear. The woman put a rough red hand to her mouth and hurried off. "You . . . got a . . . nice little . . . wife there," said the shaking man, his shoulders convulsive without laughter, his voice crackling with interference.

"Her? My wife? Are you kidding? That's Mrs. Grimes, my housekeeper. You don't see me getting hitched up like some horse, no sir. Not that I got anything against marriage, don't get me wrong. I think it's fine—for the other guy if you know what I mean. That's Mrs.

Grimes, my housekeeper. She keeps house for me. I don't mind telling you I could get a better cook and bottle washer for what I'm paying her but I feel kind of sorry for her, you know what I mean? Where would the poor woman go? What would she do?"

"You got . . . a nice . . . little house . . . keeper there," said the shaking man. "A nice . . . fine looking . . . woman."

"I don't care a hoot about that. So she does her work and knows where we stand." The blind man laughed. "I'm not one of those foolish guys who hires a woman on her looks. No sir. I don't think much of a man who does that. You can't mix business with pleasure, you know, and expect to make it in this world."

The blind man got off at the stop before David's and David, heart beating madly, decided to follow him off. He followed him to the intersection and across the street after Corky braced the blind man against a green light. He followed as the blind man went into a department store across the street, and waited to see if he would come out. After a moment he emerged with a steel guitar slung across his chest and carrying a folded canvas camp seat. One arm hugged a large tin cup at the armpit. The blind man opened the camp seat, unslung the guitar, and sat down. He hung the cup somehow on his chest and was open for business. His first song was "Say You, Say Me" and he sang the words while he picked at the guitar strings. His voice, still without timbre, seemed not quite so loud in the open air and even a little timid among the traffic noises. Without timbre his voice had a deadly, monotonous persistence and David knew he would go on singing for as long as he had to, without a crack in the enameled vocal cords. David shook himself impatiently, not liking what he felt, not happy with the blind man off the bus, and he hurried off to work to the sounds of "On the Road Again."

To the bird lady, the blind man said, "Did you happen to watch television last night, ma'am?"

"No I didn't."

"Well I did and let me tell you they're going to have to do something about this violence on television. Believe you me, it just isn't right for our kids to grow up watching people machine-gunned from black sedans or bombs thrown into laundry shops. Why this one program last night, first off these hired gunmen chop down a man in a restaurant with a sawed-off shotgun, then they run a car off a cliff with a drugged girl in it, and as if that wasn't enough, a guy gets thrown into a stall with a crazy horse that kicks him dead. I say we got to put a stop to shows like that. Did you happen to see it last night?"

The bird lady's eyelids fluttered. Her *Reader's Digest* slipped from her lap to the floor and she rushed to pick it up. "No, I'm afraid not," she said. "I don't watch television."

"I see what you mean and I guess you're right. If more people were like you and put their foot down about watching shows like that, they'd stop putting them on and we could have a lot more wholesome entertainment, something for the whole family to enjoy. People got to stop being goshdarn lazy and write their congressmen when they watch a program filled with violence and bloodshed like the one I saw last night."

David sits at the counter in the coffee shop. In the mirror behind the counter he spies the blind man, dressed in a black, tight double-breasted suit and Homburg hat, carrying a sawed-off shotgun, enter and sit down at a table. The blind man tips back his hat with the barrels of the gun and without even taking aim, pulls the triggers. Two flags pop out. One reads, THE BLIND MAN'S BOOK STORE, and the other, EVERYTHING MUST GO. Corky trots in wearing a green, body-hugging sweater which declares in red letters OUR LEASE HAS NOT BEEN RENEWED. The blind man reaches into his coat pocket and pulls out the eleventh edition of the encyclopedia, volumes one through thirty-two, worn and shedding flakes of cover but still serviceable. He reaches in again and unloads a set of Balzac, complete except for a missing volume twelve. Soon books are piled on all the tables and still they keep coming and David thinks it is certainly a shame that the blind man's lease has not been renewed and everything must go. David offers to buy a dog-eared copy of *The Minimal Self* but Corky snarls and bites him in the leg.

The beauty queen sat next to the blind man and smiled at Corky sitting with his sharp ears up, sniffing. "Isn't he *cute*?" said the beauty queen in a thin, stylish voice. "May I pet him?"

"You go right ahead, ma'am," said the blind man. "Corky's a good dog. He likes to be petted."

Pat, pat, went the beauty queen and looked at her delicately royal hand in awe. "I thought," she said, "that you weren't supposed to."

The blind man boomed his laugh. "Ma'am, that's just an old wives' tale although it may be true of some dogs, I guess. Some dogs, I guess, are like some people. You know what I mean? They're just ornery and don't like to be touched and that's probably where the idea got started. You take Corky now. He's not happy unless he thinks people are making all kinds of fuss over him so you go right ahead. You got yourself a dog of your own, ma'am?"

The beauty queen was busy rubbing her hand with a lace handkerchief. Her skin was milk white under bouffant auburn hair, and she wore an ice-blue wool dress that hugged her breasts and thighs with general satisfaction, ending just above her silken knees. "Yes, I have a lovely little dog named Schatzie," said the beauty queen. "She's a darling."

"That's good, real good, ma'am. Did you happen to see the statistics in the Humane Society journal?"

The beauty queen looked with some alarm at the blind man. "No, no, I'm afraid I didn't."

"Only one out of fifty burglaries in houses with dogs, yes ma'am. A dog's a good thing to have around in this day and age when it's not even safe to walk the streets anymore and you never know when you'll wake up to find some doped-up kid stealing you blind, yes ma'am. Is your Schatzie good with your kids? Corky's gentle as a lamb around kids, you can bet on that."

"I don't have children. I'm not married."

"Well then I beg your pardon, ma'am, but don't you worry one little bit. You know what they say, that marriages are made in heaven and that there's a man for every single woman. You just wait and see if your Prince Charming don't come along some day when you least expect it."

The beauty queen shot the blind man a scornful look and flashed a breathtaking smile around the bus. She crossed her elegant legs. "I do certainly hope so," she said.

"You'll see. Just when you least expect him, that young Prince Charming will come right along. Don't say I didn't warn you."

And David riding his white stallion with waving golden mane leaps from the saddle and loops the reins around the fireplug in front of the church. He waits until the blind man in his cutaway and the beauty queen in her wedding gown emerge from the church, then reaches into worn-smooth levis for the rice. The beauty queen laughs and ducks but the blind man walks, chin up, through the spray. David follows their bullet-proof black sedan on his horse to their hideaway apartment. He waits while the blind man informs his housekeeper that she is no longer wanted, she's through, and commandeers her apron for the beauty queen. He watches while the beauty queen dusts the floor and removes cinders from the fireplace, prepares hot tea with lemon in it for the blind man before the violent television, set in his slippers-and-smoking-pipe ways. When the blind man finally closes his eyes and falls asleep in his chair, David takes Corky's paw in one hand and the beauty queen's slim fingers in the other and leads them silently away. They gallop off, and the white stallion with the golden mane and David and the beauty queen and Corky live happily ever after.

Through no fault of his own, David sat in the blind man's place. Due to a downtown sale day, every seat was taken. He wasn't even quite conscious of where he was until the bus stopped and he saw the plump little housekeeper nudge the blind man forward. Corky and the blind man trotted up the two steps with their usual marvelous agility, the blind man dropped the precise change into the box and made his quarter turn to the left. He bumped into David's knees and David carefully examined the gleaming black policeman's shoes. He studied his own with the cracks in the leather. "Do you mind? That's my place," said the blind man.

David waited with dread for the blind man's elastic hips automatically to revolve and deposit him on David's lap. David could not move, he could not—it wasn't a matter of will—and so he would begin a new career of ventriloquist with the ONE AND ONLY blind-man dummy. Welded together prenatally, they would travel the circuit and the blind man would wow them with "A penny saved is a penny earned" and "A rolling stone gathers no moss." They would be famous because no one else would ever get the proverbial last word. "That's my place," said the blind man.

The blind man stood with his *lederhosen* knees braced against David's. "That's my place," he repeated again and again, a wound-up blind-man doll with one phrase in his clockwork. "First come, first served," said David in a sweat and held stubbornly to his place. "That's my place," said the blind man, voice trembling with timbre, and David, feeling heredital roots anchoring him to the seat, was convinced that the blind man and he would be postured so, in the midst of a gathering gaggle of tongues clucking against teeth, for all eternity, or, at least, until the matter was referred to the proper agency, or, at least, until the matter was referred to his wife, Phyllis, who, as was her custom, would never forgive him.

III

HIS DAYS ARE AS GRASS

Looking at his watch, Solon Pepper walked slowly away from the Charles River toward Harvard Square. He carefully buttoned his topcoat around his chin. It was as though he must protect the lump at the hollow of his throat and, inevitably, as he thought of it, his fingers tested the area. He gulped and the soft mass moved under his pressure. It was there, it was part of him, silent, painless, inert, and, in his twenty-third year, it might be death. It had to come out, for it might be, underneath its phlegmatic pulp, waging grim war, sucking, was it iodine? from the heart of his existence, needing what he needed and taking it over his fallen corpuscular forces—yes, part of anybody's humor today must be scientific. He was living in the age of miracles, only now they were logically positive and therefore miracles of human achievement rather than ignorance. Crossing on foot the Ocean of Storms rather than the Red Sea, that sort of thing. What did nature have to do with labels?

He crossed with the light and entered the Yard. He had a lump in his throat and he was ready to believe in God's red seas. Dear God, make my lump go away and I will forever Hail. Fear makes cowards and cowards made gods, yes even unto the last cabala if the lump would go away. He felt for it, it was still there. He gulped and it moved.

He was touched truly that his sister Phyllis had come to him from St. Louis with her marital problems and only mildly interested in the irony that she should have turned to him at the moment her crisis intersected his: troubles came in bunches, every thought he had these days was cliché, which convinced him as well as anything could that he was closer to the sense of things than he had ever been. Law escaped out one window as matters of life and death bounded in another. It was so easy to pretend, even to oneself, that the wilderness had been beaten back, the trees cleared, stumps burned, Indians stuffed into Sears-Roebuck suits, hands of fastest gunmen chopped off; easy to sit in front of a log fire while one's thumb twirled the gas thermostat and sleet rattled futilely against brick walls; easy until some busy little bodies, fierce as the Old West, created inside wildernesses. A lump.

Phyllis had fled from the ivy-covered house in the west end of St. Louis, from the enigmatic, pipe-nursing husband, from her nosy dachshund. Solon's first impulse, when she had flung herself on his bed and, in monotone, annihilated three years of marriage, was pleasure, which he immediately stifled, knowing that her failure could be pleasing to him only in terms of his own. And this struck him as extremely odd, that the possible failure of his body should be *his* failure, as if he should strap on a gun belt and face the enemy on a parched main street of throat. But this was an adversary who didn't fight fair. A laugh, an anthropomorphic one: as if human beings fought fair.

"So," he had said, "you've simply packed up and left him."

"No," she said. "I've simply left him without packing up." She smiled, twisting her thin legs around each other like strands of rope, troubling him with the exposure of lean sisterly thighs. "There's a difference. I never leave home without making sure I have my key. I might want to get back in. I told David I needed a small vacation so I would fly up to see my little untethered brother in Cambridge. No tears, no fuss, and here I am."

It was already past midnight and they, well she, had been talking for hours in Solon's small bedroom with the mustard-colored wallpaper and grimy windowsills spattered with mouse turds. The windows faced other windows across a narrow courtyard and Solon was often watched by a red-haired man and his wife. They never spoke to each other when they met downstairs but, rather, acknowledged their clandestine relationship with quickening glances before their heads turned away. Solon felt that he knew these people infinitely better than those he was presumed to know well, simply because there was a single line of communication. Multiple networks fouled the footpaths. He sat in his straight-backed wooden chair and watched his sister, trying to concentrate, trying not to fondle his throat. He had decided not to tell her.

He took off his shirt and started on his trousers. They were not modest before each other, merely uneasy. "Let's see," she said and he noticed that her uneven, ironical croak was back. Her voice was marvelous, always had been, as though the vocal cords had been damaged and then too hastily repaired, and he had always thought that she had adapted her personality to match the voice but didn't quite carry it off. "It's the sameness, I think, the whiteness of mind," she said. "A beautiful intellectual whiteness. Nothing moves. He must have the usual arsenal of emotions but they lie frozen, waiting. He won't, or can't, make his move. He loves me oddly, I'm sure of that, without overt act, and that's the way it is."

Solon went to the closet and pulled out his pajamas. They were blue with black stripes and he hesitated a moment before putting them on for they were wrinkled and very dirty. Her talk about her husband, his brother-in-law, was, of course, unfortunate, because it was, to put it simply, dull. He sat on the side of the bed and took her hand. Her strong fingers surprised him by their passivity and he realized that she considered her problem to be serious.

"No overt act. Divorce, then?" he said and remembered to squeeze her hand. She withdrew it with her bird nose wrinkled. "Pfeugh. Don't you ever wash? You stink to heaven."

He was terribly annoyed. "I don't smell anything."

"No," she said, bringing a pillow to her face and muffling the words. "Get away." He got up and sat in the wooden chair and glowered. "My God," she said relentlessly. "Just like the east side stockyards. You're hog butcher to the world."

He hated her so much that he thought of throwing her out of the apartment. She stared at his face and then smiled grimly in a way he had learned to dread: she, unlike him, once she made up her mind, remained firm, and it took apologies from many directions, spokes running to her hub, to sway her. Why was she so much more indomitable? When they were children, he would pick her up in all the glory of his incipient manhood and fling her across the room and she wouldn't cry. "It's maddening to be sympathetic and have my pajamas stink."

"They do and you're not."

"All right, they do and what am I not?"

"You're not sympathetic. That's easily beyond you. You can only pretend to be. Remember I knew you when and I know you now. Do you think I'm here for your sympathy, that I'm that naïve? I'm here for your pretense, which shows how close to the bottom of my barrel I am." She sat up, Buddha-like over narrow, crossed legs and said monotonously, "I should have known better than to come to you, shouldn't I? Your sympathy's always in hock to yourself and I don't care to redeem it anymore. You're as unbearingly selfish as ever. I'm going to a hotel."

He was ready to tell her that he had a lump in his throat. He would place her long fingers on it and she would feel it move. Of *course* he was solipsistic Sol, but that defined cancer victims, he had a right to be and it hurt him that she couldn't tell the difference, search out and destroy the anguish eating away at him. He couldn't tell her for then the difference would no longer exist. The center of his self would no longer have that tang of uniqueness. He pressed hard against his closed eyelids and invited pain, the earned kind he could endure. In a moment his head ached.

"Don't act so bruised," she said. "I won't go to a hotel." But he still wouldn't forgive her freedom from malignancy and arched his throat at the ceiling. He noticed for the first time that imprinted upon the sluggish white paint were stars of varying sizes. There were a couple of white patches as though mobiles had once been pasted on. "You," he recited, "who never ran away even from our crummy childhood, from our church-mouse poor, illiterate parents, have run away, want to learn from the sound "David Stein" makes on the polysyllabic Harvard air whether you should abandon him to his silences. For you, the stubborn, fiercely loyal one, the word keeper, only failure and humiliation awaits you in the divorce court, don't I know you as you know me? I may not care to know you as much, more likely may not be able to, but that's an entirely different matter, isn't it, from knowing? Family solidarity is all that's left of dignity in modern society, and look how outdated that is. You've come to me for assurance that this is so, and all I can offer is a sampling from the clutch of erotic visions where I live. Listen: I know a girl so beautifully put together that my throat muscles tighten when I look at her. Look at her is all. She's slim and curved, with fantastically articulated legs and breasts. Everything smoothly rounded with no lumps. No lumps at all. She has soft, large, lovely brown eyes and an adorable nose."

"Are you trying to say in your revolting rococo style," said Phyllis, "that you have no time for me because you have time for only one woman in your life? That you have found someone stupidly insane enough to be your girl?"

"Exactly so," said Solon. "My one and only. We're going to get married and live happily ever after just like you," and grew angry all over again. "There's nobody, as you damn well know. Flesh and blood are lousy ingredients for cooking up a dream girl." Indeed there was literally no one, at least since the appearance of the thyroid lump. Unless, which he didn't, you counted his well-wrought mail-order romancing of Mary Castle, the rich, gorgeous, ingenuous all-American toy princess "back home."

"I don't believe you," said Phyllis. "You always have a girl. Is she Jewish for Mom and Pop?" and Solon, regardless of the irony, was so furious at Phyllis having, under any conditions, to utter such an absurdity, that he burst into a paroxysm of laughter: the legacy from Jewish mother to atheistic daughter that preserved Judaism as no ethical or religious system could. Hebraic ears were stuffed with cotton in the womb not the synagogue. His girls were never Jewish, except for improbable ones like Mary Castle, and each time Phyllis would write, as she choked on tribal laughter, But isn't there that slight strain, that twinge, that hereditary hum, that tiny shiver of apprehension down the spine? And Solon would snap back, And isn't David so wonderful, king of Jews, so free and easy, so complete an answer to a maiden's prayers? And she would answer, having safely bagged him once again, with the unanswerable answer, since its subject swallowed its predicate, But my dear Solon, he's Jewish.

"All right, you force me to confession. There is indeed a girl and I'm madly in love and you'll never get me to tell you her name."

"Madly in love," said Phyllis. "Now of course I believe you that there is no girl. Love to you is a bundle of reasons wrapped around with a blue ribbon of synthesis. You memorize love, and that's why I'm as close to love as you'll ever get because you've rehearsed me the longest." She paused as if tired of going on. "You might have learned to love Mom and Pop if only they'd been rich and famous instead of just plain folks who love you without reservation. I've decided you're much worse than David in his worst moments. He is capable of love. He loves me. I guess it isn't his fault that he loves me in the worst way."

The two of them invariably exhausted each other. For a time, when both of them were at Harvard on scholarships, she a senior and he a freshman at the college, they studiously stayed out of each other's way, both agreeing they couldn't survive both Harvard and themselves at the same time. Then she had met that button-eyed law student who was now her husband and, after ridiculing him for months, had married him and gone back to St. Louis for good. He had no roots elsewhere and who could withstand Phyllis with a full head of steam? Her only answer to Solon's perplexed *why*'s, why she had married David, why she had gone back to St. Louis and their parents, was "Why not? Isn't it what every good Jewish girl wants, to please her parents? To present them with a nice Jewish Harvard lawyer for a son-in-law? and when she couldn't stop laughing he knew that he had finally and truly lost her, not particularly to David Stein but to his own understanding, that she was escaping him and that could very well have been her reason for going. God knew the only reason he would go back to St. Louis, his parents, hadn't been born yet.

Yet here she now was, offering him another chance, and he was scouring his memory to discover what that chance might be, and he was fumbling whatever ball he was supposed to be carrying, only worse, because he was afraid for his own hide, and the beautiful mechanism for self-absorption that was his second skin refused to let him be. He could save himself by trying, or at least wanting to try, to save her, by pushing to the forefront for once her necessity, her anguish. Was death in his throat so much more compelling *sub specie eternitatis* than the dying of her heart? People's throats died every day, hearts more rarely, was that true? He couldn't honestly say since he knew so very little about hearts.

Solon turned the corner of Mellon Street and crossed the courtyard to his apartment. He looked toward the windows of the redhead and his wife but the shades for once were drawn. He had never made a serious effort to find out what the man did, whether he was "university" or not. He didn't want to know anything about him, not really, or about the wife, as a matter of fact, that he didn't already know.

Phyllis was dressed and reading a book. He marveled at how nice she could look without being good-looking, at least, good-looking as he defined it. It was a matter of control of her material. She was wearing a soft wool brown sweater and black pleated skirt. "I've made your day," he said. "My clothes are tumbling around at the laundromat."

She put down her book and stood up. "You certainly have made my day. Let's take a walk."

"I just took a walk," he said, "to the laundromat. And I have to go back to the laundromat in an hour. You can walk with me then."

"I don't want to then, I want to now. And I can't abide laundromats. They're too steamy, like armpits of long-distance runners."

He said hopelessly, knowing that his will was no match for hers,

"It's ridiculous of you, to expect me to walk between walks. Once, just once, be reasonable with me."

"I'll go alone then. I understand perfectly. I'll see you later," and she started for the door.

"All right, all *right*," he said and smacked a fist into his palm. Once, in his childhood, he had run his fist experimentally through a pane of window glass and almost bled to death. Until then he had had an almost insane desire to bleed to death, to experience the whiteness of it all remaining, but that skirmish cured him. Now, whenever he could, he avoided the sight of blood. His suicide would be clean: poison, perhaps, or by hanging. That would be nice, the heels gently swaying an inch above the floor, the penis standing tall. But any suicide simply wouldn't do. No one fell upon his sword anymore, not even, he suspected, the Japanese with all their honor deflected into the electronic marketplaces. If the lump were in earnest, he would have to give the whole matter further thought. A fellow law school drudge had recently jumped off the Mystic River Bridge, and he remembered how ridiculously romantic the bridge's name had sounded, something that his pen pal Mary Castle would go ga-ga over. There wasn't anything ultimately to die for, though, and certainly not Law Review, just nothing to live for. One slowly circling pool and total oblivion, one final rehearsal.

They walked down the stairs and through the courtyard and met the red-haired man and his wife coming in, and he passed them with a quick, mute exchange of intimacy.

"Who are they?" said Phyllis. "They seem to know you."

"Just people who live across the courtyard. We watch each other undress."

"And you don't give that luscious homebody another thought, right?"

Phyllis actually laughed aloud and he thought how strange it was to have already forgotten her laugh. He felt piqued as though his last remaining faith had been violated, and he insisted, truly shocked at the idea, that he had never looked at the wife with any sense of lust and it was with sorrow that he realized he had been describing *her* in his "erotic vision." Had the whole unspoken, unmediated relationship with the couple, which he had regarded as a virtuous attachment, been simply another of his sexual brainstorms confined to quarters? He perversely refused to believe it and preferred to think that he was simply being knocked about by a willful sister.

"Where would you like to walk?" he said.
"Anywhere. Anywhere at all. I'm just trying to think things through. I think better on my feet. So far I haven't gotten anywhere." She was giving him another chance, openly, without a trace of her usual ironic tone, which showed him again how vulnerable she was. No more the white face and tight lips when in trouble. No more the sister of the long arms, ready to absorb his slightest whim of torment while never confessing to any of her own. She was waiting for *his* bosom, *his* strength, *his* advice, and incredibly enough, *his* will; but instead of making for shore with her in tow, he grimly treaded water. But was he so wrong to play it by his book, the only book he had learned by heart? What, after all, was the problem? People got divorced every day, no sweat, at least half of those who got married in the first place, or every night they slept with spouses they didn't love. It was the way of the Western world and the Western world went on, still busy with missile sites and terrorist hijackings and bombings and nightly business reports and all the other tuneless whistlings. But *he* might be dying. Before her very eyes, the busy little strangers in Homburg hats and tight black coats straddled his thyroid. And if he refused to listen to her problem, at least wasn't he nobly withholding the pain of his own? Never before had he spared her. She had taken every full load of his right between the eyes, and now, at the penultimate incident, wasn't he finally proving himself capable of heroism, watered-down negative though it might be? He had told her so *much*, only her. When he was eight, his "gang" had stripped him in a garage and, although this was a ritual visited on each of them in turn, he had fought and twisted until he became a special challenge, and their victorious laughter was merciless. He wore a hernia belt in those days and the shame of being exposed was unbearable. He committed the unpardonable sin of boyhood, he cried, and they threw back his pants, and he went and told Phyllis, who, he gave her full credit, never told on him.
When he was ten, his friends and he were playing in the pasture behind the rope factory. The pasture was dense with trees and enormous weeds. Great stalks, perfect spears, grew in abundance and they had wars with these spears. He was lying in ambush when a stranger, a man, seized him from behind and proceeded to violate him. The memory of the man's face, lips squirming like newborn puppies, remained with him. He told Phyllis and she, a teen-aged girl, not his helplessly inarticulate parents, had comforted him. Everything, puberty, sex, lies, his millions of deceits, she knew everything and, he

realized with a drooping, listless heart, about her he knew almost nothing and still couldn't, or wouldn't, listen. Why couldn't he hear her, at least her, out, and take his fobearance out on others? Was it the lump? Partly, but, and this was the God's truth, also because he preferred not to think of her as unhappy. Her happiness meant something to him, even if not as much as his own unhappiness. Just thinking of a god right with his heaven was surely more important than being there oneself.

He made a prodigious effort as they walked through the Yard past Widener Library. "Look," he said. "He has committed no outrageous act. He's a steady provider, he has no other women I presume, he doesn't drink too much, he is reasonably generous, kind, or so I've been told, has his teeth and hair. What more is there?"

"What more is there?" Phyllis flung out her arms. Even in the bulky cloth coat they were thin as needles. "There's the nibbling at the communal bread. After dinner we sit and wait, for what? For interruption, for something and somebody to give us a free ride. When I poke around about his law cases, he smiles infuriatingly as if to imply I wouldn't understand, not really, which of course I wouldn't because I don't care enough, and when I bring up Derrida or Barthes, who are totally and completely beyond his depth of course, he looks at me with grave and glorious contentment as if to say, 'My dear, do play with your infantile conceits. As for me, I don't deconstruct, I don't *do* deconstruction, but I'm happy you can keep yourself busy.' Everything between us *is* between us. Everything runs by implications that neither of us implies." Phyllis' voice had risen, she was strident, and it was clear that she hadn't talked about David before to anyone. This would be so. Solon knew his sister to be proud and even as he appreciated his own importance to her, the value of being the only person on earth in whom another person could confide, he became impatient. If only her problems weren't so dull, so repetitious. Did she have any idea of how many times her sisters in misery were confiding to a nation on talk shows, how hopelessly outdated Nora Helmer and her slamming doors were? All women had to do to become "little" again was to learn how horrible becoming men was.

They had passed through the Yard and were walking along the row of bookstores. "Would you like to go in and look around for a while?" he asked, vaguely aware that he was trying to distract her, not for her sake but for his own. He had discovered all over again, from a past of all-over-agains, that he couldn't bear to listen, that he was "hard of listening," for, rather than relieving, it doubled the pressure of his own tensions. What had the doctor said, what had the benightedly moon-faced doctor said? "I wouldn't worry. There is a only a fifty-fifty chance of malignancy." And then smiled in triumph at having reduced the problem to an immortal statistic. To the same trivial odds as divorce. He was a full-time man at the medical school and hadn't been educated in the art of nuance. Solon was a walking statistic, nothing more. Fifty percent of this and something percent of that and even if the doctor himself got an amalgam of cancer, bubonic plague, and multiple sclerosis the very next day, he would smack his lips over the statistics. Solon was definitely not a scientist. He was a jellied mass of as-yet-unreified law student and refused to look in a ledger for his name.

Phyllis was not interested in looking at books. She had miraculously gotten him to listen, or at least pretend to, and she refused to believe that he would now turn her off; she went on grinding out metallic bands of misery. He chose a brief pause in her recital to smile gently. "Let's take a coffee break. A little espresso? There's a brand new shop right here, see? *Espresso, au lait, cappuccino,* you name it. And coffee-house paintings on the wall. Come on. It'll do you good."

She turned grim. "Is that what I've become to you, a tourist?" and in her indignation he saw the voyeur he had become, with the world's largest anomie at his center to make up for the lump in his throat, for he spent every afternoon sipping espresso, brooding at a wall but not conscious of the wall or its paintings or even his lump, only of the possibility that a pretty girl might be admiring his clean profile and be moved by his impending tragedy. His lump became a celebration, something for a beauty queen to guess at and be dazzled by.

Phyllis allowed him to steer her into the shop and they both drank espresso in demitasse cups. Phyllis took a sip and made a face: "At least it isn't laced with cyanide, but, I know, think of the atmosphere." She eyed him forbiddingly, her lips tightened and he saw the Phyllis of his childhood. "For Christ's sake," she said. "Stop playing to the gallery. Talk to me. I've come twelve hundred miles to chat and I'm your one and only sister. Talk to me."

It was true. The moment they had come in, he had caught sight, at another table, of a girl with smoky, involved hair, straight eyebrows and quick gray eyes. She was very pretty and sitting alone. He wanted her terribly, wanted to be with her, tell her all about the lump, what was it that he was trying to tell her that he couldn't tell Phyllis? Strong and silent Solon: the term, pinned on his lapel, shriveled and turned yellow. It, he, was laughable and just wouldn't do. Tell, tell, tell all, tell them all, let then wrap the soft, sweet arms around and bury the sweating head on the absorbent, absorbing breasts. Tell to the stranger who would be kind, who didn't care enough to be unkind.

"I don't know what you're talking about," said Solon, and his eyes made it perfectly clear that he did, lingering lovingly on the girl. Even as they both watched her, she got up and walked out. He noticed with real disappointment that she moved awkwardly, was shaped not at all well. He lost interest and was annoyed at his sister's fretful smile. "You haven't changed a bit, haven't grown up at all," she said. "You take nothing that isn't handed to you wrapped and beribboned and you want nothing that isn't impossible. You live a nice, warm existence wrapped in your glittering, tinseled, wretched myths." She glared at him until he fell to fondling his spoon, coated with espresso. "I wonder," she went on, "what made me think that you might help me, that you might possibly help anyone. I couldn't really have been so desperate that I borrowed one of your illusions, could I?" She meditated. "Perhaps I saw something, some slight something, in your letters, I don't know, but if so, whom did you get to write them? I've decided, Sol, to fly back to St. Louis tomorrow, not to David necessarily, just back. Just away from your loving caring."

He knew this Phyllis very well. This was the old Phyllis. It had come to this: if he didn't tell her about the lump she would leave convinced that they had nothing left for each other, that a lifetime of childhood and adolescence together failed before one simple test of sympathy. If he told her, it might make absolutely no difference. She had every right to assume, as he did, that he cared not quite enough for her, for her problems, that he casually exhausted her feminine sensibilities and repaid her with masculine indifference. All of this was very well true, but when she learned of his matter of life and death, wouldn't it be understandable enough for one more forgiveness? It had to be weighed against his chivalric vow of silence. All his life he had blabbed to her and he had sworn this time to carry the whole bloody weight of suffering by himself. He couldn't assume her burden, not with his god-given chain of genetic beads, but at least he could carry his own, couldn't he?

Think of the possibilities. If he confessed the lump, might not her own troubles dwindle and perhaps even vanish in an incidental shrugging off of a husband she obviously had no love for, for the sake of a brother whom she had loved through thick and thin for many years, to whom she had committed a large part of her girlhood? Sacrifice, for a woman, justified any action. Love over honor for millions of women any day, Ibsen had said. Phyllis could easily throw over the world, she was strong enough, but only for someone she loved, not like a man who could pitch it all for an idea. Well, he had an idea. His idea was simple. To be a man he had to carry the lump in silence. The simplicity of the idea intoxicated him. He was a drunkard who had never had a drink before.

He stood up. "Let's go," she said. "I've truly decided to go back, but it has absolutely nothing to do with you. You can believe that. You're not nearly as bad as both you and I think you are." Something in her pronouncement moved her, and she began shaking her head, and couldn't speak for a moment. Finally she delighted him, as if she'd read his thoughts, by getting out, "Solon, you're such an abysmally simple man."

As they left the coffee shop, Phyllis said impatiently, "Do you know you have a tic? You keep fondling your throat like a dowager with beads."

Solon dropped his hand instantly and tried to look wise behind a giggle. "It's not a habit, just a tumor," he said.

"Very funny. So why ain't I laughing?"

And Solon, turning toward her set profile, examining her curved nose and gaunt frame, finding in each familiar feature the unfamiliarity of his newfound restraint, was moved by her in a new, bitter way, moved because he, finally, however briefly, was hurting her in order not to pain her, because he, finally, however briefly, understood that when one treated love with the respect due to strangers, one loved. "Don't go on like this," he managed to get out. "Please. I care about you. I just don't quite know what it means to care. Please. I'm not as bad as you and I think I am."

She could only shake her head. "Solon, you're becoming quite a stand-up comedian. Forget it. You'll never make it. You don't know how to be bad any more than how to be good. You're not programmed for that sort of thing. Never were and never will be. You're too thoughtless to be bad and too heartless to be good." She shook her head definitively, and this time he knew he was being dismissed, that class was out. "I don't think you're bad at all."

IV

DEAR DAYS

Dear Solon,

After a very dreary day of attending classes at the university, it was quite refreshing to find your letter waiting for me. You see, short though it was, I was very glad that you did write.

Your modesty overwhelms me, as I've had no suspicion as to your fierce spirit not being a sincere one. I must assure you that my opinion of you is merely in the embryonic stage, and you can develop it in any way you choose. Ahem! I'm getting into deep water! What I mean is that by a mutual correspondence we can both reveal our unknown qualities. I find this rather exciting as I've never written to anyone on so slight an acquaintance, which gives me an opportunity to expound my ideas without the slightest notion of whether they coincide with yours. In this way I shall be utterly honest and never say things merely to be agreeable.

Tell me a little of your life there at law school and your routine. Have you settled down again to your studies after your vacation? You may try all my cases and be the supreme judge. Every time I walk into the law library at the university, I get a sudden desire to study law, but that's as far as it goes. The rehearsals at school for the play I'm in keep me rather occupied. They keep telling me that if I keep plugging, I may show a little talent *some*where!

I've tried in a most unsuccessful way to say, "Please write me often!" Gee, that was easy. I'll now continue trying to gain some knowledge of the causes of the Fall of Rome, so until next time,

As always,
Mary

Dear Solon,
   To begin with, as I told you before, I am pursuing the theatre at school. My big opportunity for stealing the show was when I entered all decked out in a sexy black nightgown and said coyly, "How do you like my new creation?" At which point the audience was expected to swoon. But—at rehearsal, the director shouted, "Cut that out! She won't be able to change fast enough." Naturally I assured him of the speed with which I could dress and undress, but to no avail.
   Of all my classes, I believe that I enjoy public speaking the most. Wednesday, I was to give a report and I prepared it thoroughly only to wind up in catastrophe. I faced the class and opened my mouth to pour forth bits of wisdom but, to my horror, no words came out! Still worse, the room began to sway, whence I ran out to the ladies' room and proceeded to lose my breakfast. What a riot I caused!
   Seriously though, Solon, I enjoyed your letter and found myself bursting into peals of laughter. You really touched my funny bone and should consider that quite an achievement as I rarely laugh aloud when reading. I am sending you one of my lyrics of love and know you will think I am hyper-sensitive, frustrated, or something, but come what may, the thoughts are my own and written with deep sincerity. You will probably tell me it's too long and you will be right, but please understand that it was written spontaneously—the thoughts flowed out through the medium of a pen. Hope your criticism won't be too harsh! Well, Solon, I know you must be weary or something, so I'll just say, "Write soon."

Yours,
Mary

My dear, dear Sol,
   I am sitting in the most peaceful place. Your guess is correct—the law library. Supposedly I am working on a theme but you are a study much more enjoyable. There I go again!
   The past week has been full of excitement: I appeared in *three* one act plays! Look for my name in lights on Broadway! All three plays were rather awful but I *am* getting a real glimpse into the life of an actress, as it was grabbing a meal here, running off to the theatre there, no sleep, living every line, acting on and off stage—I've just returned to normalcy. I shall never forget Monday night, the rehearsal at which, after making the most poised entrance imaginable, I

tripped and fell flat on my face! To my surprise I jumped up and carried off my *few* lines like a veteran. The real fun was back-stage, where people "let down" their hair.

The week before last I spent every afternoon pursuing higher knowledge, mainly because of an exam. Accomplishing five weeks work is rather difficult in one week. Trials and tribulations of a young college student often burden me with too much thought. As you are aware, I, too, am a thinker. I say "too" because I know that you are a very deep person and are often lost in clouds of thought. Which statement brings me to the next section—

Yesterday was a wonderful fall day and I had a perfectly beautiful experience. Dressed informally I went to the park and sat by the lake, watching the birds fly freely overhead. My solitude was unbroken for three hours and it was in this spot that I realized the truth of God's omnipotence. I could almost *feel* the breeze kissing the trees. How seldom people relax! It's only on days like these that I feel at peace with the world.

I envied your treat of muscatel wine, cheese and crackers, and want you to let me do that with you sometime. You, your friend, Charlie (he's called me several times just to chat), and I could get together and talk all night. As to your poem, *Consolation,* anything I might say to describe my feeling would sound trite, but may I say, "I loved it, I was deeply moved"? It was simply beautiful and had so much meaning. Now I must admit something—I memorized it! It really requires recitation and the more I say it aloud the better it gets. This line has so much music in it: "The flickering, rollicking lick of the fire." I was speechless and motionless after reading it.

Usually I am very critical in my opinions but, honestly, Sol, I was carried away. The rhythm you achieved without rime was truly amazing.

Thus I come to the end of my letter. I have been writing intermittently all day and I really dislike saying, "Goodnite," as our communication has been so pleasant. I'm looking forward eagerly to your next letter. In lieu of anything else, I'll say, "Pleasant dreams."

Love,
Mary

Dearest, darling Solly,
So many new and exciting things have happened since you sent me

Scotty—I can't believe it's been only two days! First I want you to know how much I love Scotty and that I shall sleep with him every nite and I think he is so cute and, honey, it was *ever* so clever an idea. I adore little animals and he fits on my bed perfectly. Also *Mom* thought it was a very cute idea. Through no effort of yours, she's on your side. I think *Dad* must have said something to convince her of your various merits.

Now to add a new note. You know I decided to drop out of school for awhile and learn about the *real* world. So I got that job in the advertising agency. I want you to know that I left the agency and why. Vicki, the young gal who hired me, expected me to be and act subordinate to her, which I refused to do. By Monday afternoon, in only two weeks, I had captured the office's heart and I sensed her resentment. Around 3:30 she called me over and gave me a long tale of woe about how cramped they were for office space and that I'd have to leave, and she was *so* sorry. Also, she said my typing wasn't fast enough, whence I pounced on her, claiming she knew my speed when she hired me, which is true, and that it was unfair to hire me in the first place knowing my speed was inadequate. She beat around the bush, became flustered, and finally admitted that she thought I was too enthusiastic and made friends too fast. So, my darling, I'll have to learn to curb my exuberance.

Anyhow I was upset at this little you-know-what letting me go, so I went to see the boss and he was very sympathetic and said he was sorry it happened and hoped it wouldn't bother me, but she was jealous of me, and since I did work for Vicki, he felt it unwise to go over her head. *However,* he gave me a terrific letter of recommendation and advised me where to go first and why, and that he was sorry about the trouble and hoped I'd understand like a sport—which I did.

So I dashed to all the department stores filling out applications like mad, and I have *three* excellent prospects. Also I signed up for an evening course in Art and Arch, though I doubt if I can attend all the classes.

I received your letter today and, darling, you were magnificent. I really roared. I am so lonesome for my wonderful lover, sweetheart, companion, confidant and admirer. Write me everything.

Yours forever,
Mary

P.S. Just remember my misery in being away from you and I believe that you will beg me to visit you. *Dad likes you very much and will do anything he can to help.*

Yours forever and ever,
Mary

Darling Solly,

Although you really don't deserve a letter, as I haven't received mail from you for a whole week, the pen is acting like a magnet and I am drawn to my desk this lovely winter evening. Last night, the moon was full, the air crisp and cold, and my thoughts turned to you.

Today I saw Dr. Jamison, our family doctor, and told him of my matrimonial intentions and he wasn't at all shocked. In fact, he seemed pleased at my effervescence. He guffawed when I told him you smelled good. Remark by him: "Kiddo, you never forget a word I say." Dad also spoke with him and seemed satisfied when he came out of his office.

Your sister, Phyllis, has invited me to lunch Tuesday. I couldn't withhold the news of our marriage from her. She was all excited! Do you want to back out? Do you still love me as much as before? I am ga-ga for you, young man!

Yours forever,
Mary

P.S. Charlie came over Sunday and we walked in the park and he had to endure my constant subject of conversation—you. He said, "I hope you *do* get married, then I won't have to hear, Solly, Solly, Solly." Whence I assured him I would always talk about the man I adore and if Charlie doesn't like it, he could lump it. But I am aware that in reality he loves to hear about us.

Yours for eternity,
Mary

Dear Solon,

How to begin? Here goes: we've met Mary and naturally fell in love with her. She is the easiest person in the world to love, a child of nature, and refreshingly free of intellectual cant, which I presume is what has attracted her to you, since you're so full of it. I think I can say in all honesty and objectivity that she was quite taken with us all—yes, with Mom and Pop as well as David and me. Watching her wrap David around her little finger, I can set your mind to rest as to one hazard of the matrimonial sea: she is definitely not a lesbian. She's lovely and has the most spontaneous air of anyone I've ever known. And then again, miracle of miracles, she's *Jewish*, don't you know? Are you doing this just to please Mom and Pop, after all? Of course you are. She came over last Tuesday to Mom's for lunch simply bubbling with *joie de vivre* and danced around the room singing, "I'm the luckiest girl in the world." She informed us of her plans for a large wedding, asked me quite formally to "stand up" (where on earth did you find someone so *adorably* old-fashioned?), and I, of course, accepted as to the manor born, extending my arms and my heartfelt congratulations—even though you, in your typical fashion, haven't dropped a word to us about any marriage plans. Which is not to say that we were not, and are not, prepared to be utterly delighted at the thought that someone has managed to locate that absentee heart of yours. All right. Even though, I thought, how much more appropriate something quiet and small and dignified would be in view of the divergence of family fortunes. It's a class thing, of course, which Americans secretly deify whenever they can get away with it. You know, all those appraising country club eyes measuring the lack of total net worth of poor Mom and Pop, calculating how *lucky* the humble folk must feel to have their son lay the golden egg, or is that too indelicate for "Solon in love"? I hope so. Maybe it will prod you into a few lines of this or that, let me know how you, your frozen heart and heated gonads, stand in all this, whether you truly love her, truly love her family's fortune, what? Have you lost your scholarship and are grimly bound and determined to pull off An American Tragedy, what?

But I keep mum, being only an innocent, bystanding sister of the groom. I huddle in the dark shadows of ignorance. I assume I don't have to tell you how excited and thrilled dear, sweet Mary is. You must know, or if you don't, now you do.

The entire week she called me every day and yesterday she dropped over to visit; we sat in the kitchen talking over coffee a la soap opera, which, every now and then, forgive me, my sense of this thing blurs into. Every time I wanted to bring her down to nuts and bolts, dollars and sense (after all, I am your older sister and raised you from a pup), she would, in her infectious way, merely brush it all away with, "Things will work out. Love is a many-splendored thing (I swear). Success is written all over Solly. I'm going to work," etc., etc. I kept laughing and teasing, teasing and laughing: "What does your mother say? What does mums say? What does *Mother* say?" (Incidentally, we knew by this time that her mums had said a *very* small wedding was in order and that meeting the family wasn't necessary until *you* came in at the spring break. I say a hearty amen to the small wedding bit but must admit to good old-fashioned proletariat paranoia about the family meeting deferment. What are we, chopped liver? Frankenstein's monsters and how they grew? Does even Harvard go for naught?

It all smacks ominously of prayerfulness on the part of the Castle connection that the lace-curtain Castles may *never* have to meet the shanty-Jewish Steins at all—or am I exhibiting orthodox prickles of the upwardly mobile? My nose is truly bent out of shape (I know, literally since birth) because I have to wing this whole damn assimilation of the lifestyles of the rich and famous without the merest signal from you. What do you know of the Castles? Are they revolting, superficial prigs, as I imagine they very well might be? Parvenu for the course?

In response to my question about her mum's thought, Mary simply laughed and said I was worried over nothing and we talked of other things (She laughs and I talk. Sometimes I imagine she doesn't understand a word I say. Does this happen to you? Don't get me wrong, I am not disparaging, just envying) until I drove her home. When we arrived at her house, she asked me—I could tell it was spur of the moment—to come in and meet her mother. I didn't want to put her on the spot, after all, I might soil the furniture, so I said, "No, Mother doesn't expect me," "I'm late for the hair dresser," and so forth. Mary, however, with gathering euphoria, insisted, opining that her mother would think it queer if I didn't (I gathered her mother must look out the front lace-curtain windows a lot) so I decided to go in. It was Mary, it then developed, who was late, for a tennis engagement. She precipitously dashed out after a tremulous, "Mom, this is Phyllis, Solly's sister, she's wonderful," leaving me there alone to face her mother. I do believe, Solon, she's afraid of her mother. Perhaps it's a class thing?

Mrs. Castle and I, in our chat of about an hour, became *quite* old buddies, as if we were in the service together with awareness of ancestry temporarily suspended. Also, Mr. Castle joined us. I know you've met them briefly so you know they look and dress like Hollywood in the old days playing the upper class. I withdraw that. They're actually more decent people than I expected, who seem to be under a considerable strain about all this. I plunged in and said cautiously to Mrs. Castle in my best party voice, "I suppose congratulations are in order for both of us. Frankly, I was stunned. You know, your lovely daughter simply carries a person away with her happiness and enthusiasm."

She answered, I must say, in admirably forthright fashion, and won the first round going away. "Phyllis, my dear, as I've told Mary, I simply cannot get thrilled over this and I'm extremely skeptical about Mary's 'falling in love.' This isn't the first time, you know." I didn't know but I had this vision, Solon, of an assembly line of store-front dummies moving right along into the life and love of Mary Castle, and they all looked just like you. She continued on another tack: "I'm so happy to have you here to discuss the situation. How does Solon expect to support Mary? I'm afraid he's depending too much on Mary's working for him, or some such thing, while he finishes law school and I'm afraid he's in for a disappointment. She won't stick at it." She paused and then went for the jugular. "As for us handing over much on a silver platter, that's quite out of the question. You may not realize this but we, Oliver and I, have worked much too hard to get where we are. We've seen too many children fall completely apart with parental pampering. We want Mary to wait until Sol graduates and gets a job and shows he can stand on his own feet. Help is helpful only when it isn't necessary, that's our credo. We may seem narrow and selfish but, believe me, we're not. We will do anything for Mary and those she loves when we are convinced she is mature and responsible. As it is, we can't do anything with her. She says, simply, 'I'm twenty-one and can do as I please.' Mary tells me you are all thrilled to death. I'm sorry that I can't be."

At this point, if you can imagine this, Solon, and I'm chagrined even now to admit it, tough old bird Phyllis, your steely-eyed sister, Phyllis, begins to lump up and her steely eyes are stinging like mad so I figure I'd better talk loud and fast, strictly déclassé. "Since you've been so graciously unequivocal, I'll be the same. How could we, *petit bourgeoisie* though we are, have been 'thrilled'? Your daughter came into our house and announced her marriage. That was the first we'd heard of it. She told us the date, place and time. We said, 'Congratulations.' What are we supposed to say, go peddle your fish somewhere else, we don't do marriages in this family?"

Mr. Castle quite decently chimed in, "Yes, yes, that's true. Mary's like that." I proceeded on my mirthless way, "Solon and I have always been very close. If he intended to get married, he would have told me. It's utterly absurd that he wouldn't have told me and his parents. Have you thought of giving your daughter a lie detector test instead of setting your dogs on us?" By this time, Solon, goddammit, I completely humiliated myself and set back woman's lib a generation. My cup ran over the brim and I was bawling like a baby. These folks had made me retrogress to those childhood days when we wore patched clothing to school and the other kids laughed at us. Those stupid, talentless taunts of childhood that rend and tear the rest of our lives.

Mr. Castle, who is in grave danger of being a nice guy, said, "We had no idea that you and your parents felt as we do. I am terribly sorry to have misread you so. I am sure that Frieda (Mrs. Castle, whose hand he was holding all this time, nodded timidly at me in a most surprising, propitiatory way) agrees with me totally. We had no idea that Solon has been as uncommunicative to you as he has been to us. He has placed us in a terribly difficult and vulnerable position and now I see he has done the same with you. Believe me, I'm not trying to put him down, but the only view we have of all this is what we get from Mary and, God love her as much as we do, she does tend to embroider facts. After the failure of our first expectations of hearing from Solon, which Mary kept promising he would do, we have thought many times of ourselves contacting Solon, but were afraid of being misunderstood and permanently damaging our relationship with him . . . and Mary. Then we thought, too, surely he would say something to his own family and we would hear from them. When this also didn't happen, we became increasingly distraught. I am happy that at least some of the air has cleared and that we know that Solon's silence has not only been with us. So let's put our heads together and maybe between us we can sort the thing out. Do you think, Phyllis, you can get some news from Solon that might help us to know the true state of affairs?" He tried to smile. "A sort of corroborating witness."

I told him, Solon, that I had written you several times, urgently, with no response. Also, that I had called the law school and left word for you to call me, equally to no avail. I said that as soon as I got home I would again write you, which I am doing.

We talked for another half hour and I must confess, I rather like the Castles, or, rather, I particularly like Mr. Castle. Mrs. Castle, although she is not the horror I thought she might be, will never get a blue ribbon for tact. One of her unforked-tongue accounts was, "I asked Mary, if she's so much in love with Solon why has she continued dating other boys. Mary answered that these were dates made in advance of Solon's 'popping the question' (where is she coming from?) and were her *very last*, and that Solon knew all about it and thought she was a remarkable person for so firmly honoring her commitments. And

I said, there are commitments and commitments, and if you are so bound to Solon, that is a higher commitment for which you should break the smaller ones, and Mary just smiled radiantly and said, 'Solon knows best.'"

Do you, Sol, do you know best? Do you know anything? Are you still there or are you permanently out to lunch? Mrs. Castle further hazarded the opinion that based upon Mary's prior record of dating, she would "just have to see" Mary closing out any future dating. But of course you've discussed all that with Mary too.

On this ominous note we parted, not quite friends but not quite not friends. More like partners in crime.

Solon, I drove home still grousing at the Castles for being too rich for my blood. Yet I admit, and I keep repeating it because I find it so extraordinary under the circumstances, to a sneaking liking for the Castles in general and a passion for Mr. Castle in particular. And in at least one area, I know they are right. You should wait up or else tell us why not. You should give Mom and Pop a little dignity in their absolute pride in and love for you. They haven't slept for nights, worrying over whether they will shame you at the wedding. You've made them feel so miserably isolated and left out by not telling them a goddam thing, not even dropping a hint, much less the other shoe. They are terrified that in the final analysis they have let you down by not having been able to buy Manhattan Island for you. I'm not sure I can ever forgive you for wrapping our sweet, adoring parents around a flagpole. So talk to me, talk to them, write to me, write to them. *Get cracking*, Solon, before I sick Uriah on you.

All right, then. I've told you everything that you have a right to know, and, I expect from your point of view, much more besides, except that our horrid cousins have called to offer congratulations and simply *drool* over what a swell (i.e. rich) family you are marrying into. Wait until the Castles get a whiff of them. Talk about uncouth! I'll give you uncouth.

Love,
Phyllis

Dearest Sol,

Last Saturday I went out with Jack Clemens, one of my last dates, a lovely lad but I was bored to tears. I heaved a sigh of relief when I closed the door good-night. We went out to dinner with a married couple and I kept thinking how dull their marriage seemed and how beautiful ours will be. My own family says I'm full of surprises, so you can imagine what an exciting life we'll have together.

I went to see your sister, Phyllis, yesterday and she drove me home. I introduced her to my mother and Mom thought she was a lovely, sensible girl and was amazed how beautiful and wonderful she looks. I can't believe she's an old married lady; she looks twice as young as I, but I guess that's what being married to Mr. Right does for you. If so, I'll be running around in pinafores pretty soon, my darling. They chatted for awhile; Mom said that Phyllis thought I was adorable and that she was very happy with your choice, but was disappointed that you hadn't written your family about your marriage plans. Please do this for me. Write them a note.

Tonight I went to my night school class (Art and Arch) and afterwards Charlie, who's also in the class, took me out for a few beers and we talked only about you. I believe he is rather tired of my woeful tales of love and suffering. Tough!

I love you so much and can hardly wait for April 5, our *wedding* date!

I adore you,
Mary

Dear Solon,

This letter may be somewhat of a surprise to you. Mary has told us something of your plans. You may not be aware of it, but Mary is under a doctor's care. Because of this we ask your cooperation in discouraging Mary from considering marriage in the spring. This is very important to us.

We are hopeful that sometime in the near future she will be in a more settled state of mind so that you can proceed with your future plans. We do feel that it would be to your mutual advantage to plan your marriage for after graduation, when we can give our full blessing and cooperation.

I would like to hear from you as soon as possible.

Sincerely,
Oliver Castle

Darling Sol,

It is now midnite. I have just returned from the Symphony with Charlie, only we didn't go to the Symphony; instead we danced at the

Statler, talked about you all evening, and here I am. I received your special delivery letter and am very concerned about its contents. Dearest, believe me, I had no idea I was withholding vital information. As far as I know, I tell you everything. I was definitely shocked that my father had written you, but I must say I admired your answer tremendously. Sweetheart, you wrote him a masterpiece! In fact you have *so* impressed Mother and him. Isn't that wonderful? Darling, I love you more than I can ever hope to express and I will never, never keep anything from you. You are the one thing in life I want.

Your sweetie,
Mary

Dear Solon,
Your letter eliminated all doubt in my mind as to your really knowing Mary. Believe me, every father wants his daughter to be loved by someone with understanding and sincerity. I want you to know that I was considering you as well as Mary when I wrote. My thoughts were based on Mary's actions—dating, etc.—but you seem to know about that.

I am very relieved to hear that you have not really discussed marriage plans with Mary. She does have a way of putting words in other people's mouths. Perhaps some time after your graduation you will both know better where you stand.

Sincerely,
Oliver Castle

Darling Solly,
First, you asked about my dating. I am going out occasionally now, with Charlie, and with a young boy whose mother just passed away, so that is rather out of sympathy and makes me feel good to know I am, in my small way, helping to brighten the sudden darkness in someone's life. Anyway, I want to tell you what I decided yesterday. After writing you, I was very depressed and felt I needed to find a cure for my feelings of frustration and unhappiness. Upon talking with my Mother and Dad, we decided I should have a week's rest away from people, so I slept until one today, went horseback riding, and then to the movies *all by myself*. Last nite I read, knitted, and took a walk with Mother. Our terms are improving since I have been in more of a relaxed state. Doc Jamison also was glad I was doing this as he felt that I had been pushing myself too hard.

I am answering no phone calls for a week, not until I feel zippy again. Please don't worry, though, as there is nothing organically wrong and I am undertaking this rest cure voluntarily. I shall be in tiptop shape by the time you come home.

Also, I wish I were thinner, but I'm finding it very difficult to deprive myself of food! Can you love me still? I promise, by the time we get married on April 5, I shall once again be streamlined; it will just take a little time to groove myself. Please understand.

Darling, I am longing so to see all of my dreams of life with you become realities of sweetness and light, harshness and quarrels, peace and war, black and white, happiness and sadness—all this is marriage and I shall do everything to make you and our future happiness secure and permanent. I love you so.

Your beloved sweetheart,
Mary

Darling Sol,

After getting your letter, I feel a million times better, but I want to clarify a few things. First of all, I am not ill, I merely need several days of complete relaxation. I talked to Doc Jamison today and he wanted me to make this clear to you so that you would not worry. Really, I feel terrific. I am propped against two pillows in my dimly lit bedroom and it is pouring and thundering overhead. I love this kind of weather and only wish you were with me now, to feel the touch of my tender hands. Then I would kiss you passionately and whisper my love into your ear, pull the blanket up to my shoulders, slowly lower my nightie, and the rest is up to you—whew!

Isn't that a very unpleasant scene to look forward to in the spring? And that isn't all! I have many more secrets in store for you, which will be revealed at the proper place and time.

Since you requested that I not wear powder, I have refrained from doing this and my complexion has cleared up considerably. In fact, I've been told it's lovely and peachy—da dum!

I'm almost falling asleep, so I'll stop. I miss you.

I love you,
Mary

My darling Solly,

I do here and now believe that this rest is working wonders. I'm still overweight but I promise I shall soon be tapered down to the old

Mary. It's this hyper-emotional stage I'm going thru that makes me eat when I'm not hungry. Dearest, love me enough to bear with me until I get completely well. Doc Jamison says that this is the reaction after a near nervous breakdown. The person wants to make up for lost time and tries too hard to do too much; consequently, they get hyper this, that, and everything. I'm taking tiny capsules and I always feel better after I take one, isn't that dopey! Of course, I don't want to wind up a hypochondriac, so I'm careful not to rely on these medicinal aids.

Really, honey, I don't want you to worry because it is so unnecessary. I feel lots better already and not nearly so depressed. Your homecoming is just six weeks away and I tremble when I think that at last I shall be seeing you again and feeling your arms around me.

Last nite Charlie picked me up, we listened to records, and dropped into Town & Country, had a few drinks, talked about you and me, love and marriage, and so forth. Charlie is a doll and I'm grateful to him for letting me be his friend too. Since you've been gone, he is the only friend of yours who has called and kept in touch with me. There is no plausible reason why your other friends can't call, at least to inquire how I am. But don't say anything as it is too trivial to bother about.

Well, enough of this nonsense. I love you. I am going to take a walk and whisper my love to the winds.

I miss you—only six more weeks!

Mary

Dear Solon,

I've had an extended letter in my possession for three days, but, you must forgive me, this situation has dimensions that have turned my hair, teeth, claws, and brain puce. I simply cannot mail the letter, written by the "good, old" Phyllis, which would otherwise be long gone if the "good, old" Phyllis were still around to mail it. I suppose I owe you a debt of gratitude. You, by a reverse spin, by your total lack of precept and example, have made a better because-more-dishonest woman out of me. I've been waiting for my "reflective period," as you phrased it, to elapse, and as yet I have neither destroyed the letter nor mailed it. I will certainly never mail it but I find a certain comfort in perusing it from time to time. On balance, I've decided that there is too much in it that would hurt people (not you, I mean real people), or at the very least diminish them in my eyes by virtue of the publication of their follies, through the act of mailing. The new, puce Phyllis would by then be quite unhappy since she now understands she dislikes hurting real people.

This is all to say that I wouldn't mind very much hurting *you*, since I am still employed upon that will-of-the-wisp game of trying to get through to you where it hurts. If one pricks you, do you bleed? I've come to doubt it, Jewish blood or not. At any rate, I will quote briefly: "I probably know Mary better than anyone on earth by now. Certainly more than you who, I'm now quite sure, have no instruments for knowing people either wisely or too well. In any event, I wish you to know something of the Mary I know before that knowledge becomes mired in mud. Everything I've written about her still goes, her vivacity, ingenuousness, charm, loveliness on the one hand, her romanticism, theatricality, impulsiveness, superficiality and general lack of a decent density on the other, but *above and beyond all that* . . ." I stop here while I'm still ahead, while I still have a head. She is certainly worthy of being loved and cared for by someone who takes her mixed bag on her own terms, and on her own terms she is certainly capable of deep love and devotion. However, I'm afraid her mate will have to have an inexhaustible capacity for empathy and sympathy. I don't know anyone around like *that* on the near horizon, do you?

This letter will puzzle you, I presume. If so, you deserve every bit of it. You, being you, probably will not read between the lines. You've never been interested enough to read between the lines. In any event, this will be the last of this sort of thing. I've become emotionally involved for the both of us and, as you may recall, which I sincerely doubt, I've got a few troubles of my own. Which, being serendipitous, like all serendipities, seem to be getter smaller and smaller. Shall I thank you? No thanks.

Love,
Phyllis

My sweet darling Solly,

I've just gotten home from a party to which Dick Crowder invited me. He is a boy with an artificial leg. No need to feel *too* sorry for him however: he drives a car, makes oodles of money, and can dance marvellously. It was a dull evening but anyway I did my duty. How can you refuse a person with an artificial leg? He has been calling me for ages but I always hesitated, knowing my tendency would be to pity him. We talked about you all evening. I told him I was in love and getting married and he said that you were very fortunate as I would make a terrific wife. So there! I just read an excellent book on marriage, love, sex, and the family, by a doctor. Now my little secrets have new little ones. Hmmm! I just can't tell you before. That would take all the fun out of it. I can promise you, your life with me won't be uninteresting. Dearest, none of my clothes fit me except four dresses and two suits so I have been ransacking Mother's wardrobe. I am so excited about seeing you so soon, if only to catch a glimpse of your darling freckled face and red hair—talking about hair, wait till you see me! I wanted to look different thinking I would feel different. Well, I *do* look different and, by God, I *feel* different. Gee darling, I hope you won't mind too much. You fell in love with a brunette but you will be seeing a blonde! Just like Phyllis! Personally, I think it looks good. So do most of my friends. It may take you awhile to get used to it. I am dying to see your first reaction.

In the beginning I wasn't going to tell you. I was just going to write that I had a "new" look. In case you are curious to know what I look like, well, I am a mixture of Bo Derek and Linda Evans (when she was younger, of course)—not bad! My hair has a lovely lustre, and I look very sexy and sensuous and you will probably want to kiss me to death—at least. Sweetheart, you will be the judge, but all my life I've had a secret desire to see myself as a blonde. I got tired of looking at my fat brunette face and this blonde hair does make my face look thinner. Yesterday it had a reddish caste which my father didn't like so I had it fixed up but good.

Gosh, I never knew the agony one undergoes with a "touch up." At first it burns, then it feels cold. Oh, you go thru all kinds of dopey processes before it's all over. But enough about "Mary goes blonde," I didn't receive a letter today. I hope I get two tomorrow. Darling, I love you so. I hope you still will love me as a blonde.

I'll love you always,
Mary

My darling Solly,
    I've just returned from a delightful visit with your Mom and Pop and Phyllis and Davy. I went all dressed up for a change (I usually wear slacks). Your family likes my dazzling blonde hair. I wonder if you will. Phyllis says it makes me sparkle. Darling, I love you so. I can hardly wait.

I am getting on quite well with my parents except they don't like my new hair and are very anxious to hear what you have to say about it. I've been getting a great deal of rest—sleeping until three every day. Tough life. I haven't talked to Charlie lately, but he'll probably call in a day or so. Well, sugar-pie, I haven't received any mail for quite a few days and you just don't know how sad that makes me. *Please* write.

I love you with all
of my very full heart.
Mary

Dear Solon,
There is nothing to clarify. No doubt I suffer from "innuendo-itis" as you suggested. Or perhaps it's what as kids we used to call gaposis. Mary again spent Sunday afternoon with me and, again, we get along beautifully. The substance of any "amorphous suggestions and vague warnings," I appreciate you know all about and in your infinite awareness and empathy dismiss with a properly scornful wave of the hand. I suggest you have more correspondence with Mr. Castle. He is quite a wonderful rich-man, warm, sensitive, and intelligent. You might even learn a thing or two from him. This is your affair, after all, not mine.

Phyllis

Dearest Sol,
Why? Why? Why haven't you written me, what on earth have I done to receive such treatment? I haven't gotten mail for *days*. Have I said anything so awful? Please tell me. This silence is an endless pit of hell. I can't sleep. Why must you torture me so? Can our love be that light and airy that you feel it doesn't need constant rekindling? Here I am looking forward to seeing my loved one in a few days and what occurs? Silence. Flood of letters and then a drought. Darling, if you love me, please explain. Perhaps tomorrow will bring news. My days are miserable when I don't get a little note from you. Please don't punish me. You are my whole life. Nothing else matters.

Your love,
Mary

Dearest Sol,
First I want to apologize again and ask you to find it in your heart to forgive me. I want to thank you for allowing me to speak to you once

more before you left town. I *had* to speak. I was tormented all day. I'm sorry if Charlie or anyone else told you those things, because there is one thing which occurred that I wanted to discuss with you, but you didn't give me a chance. I am only sorry I overestimated Charlie. I thought he was a swell person, but I see now he was a serpent waiting to seduce me, and to poison your love. If he were a true friend of yours, he wouldn't have taken advantage of my loneliness. As for the others, I swear they wouldn't have happened if it hadn't been for Charlie starting it.

My parents think you are a fine boy and in a way are glad you "told me off," so to speak. But I believe you could have been more gentle and achieved the same result. Your treatment last night was very unkind. I am not reprimanding you. I am merely telling you how I feel about the whole mess.

However, you are free now and under no obligation to me. I only hope that somewhere along your road, you'll kick over a rock on which will be inscribed, "You made a mistake, Sol. You really love Mary. Go to her now." Of course, this is only wishful thinking, but I still can't get it thru my head that you don't love me at all. Well, I've said enough except that I shall fight to gain back your love and respect. If you don't want me, I'll know that from the beginning your love was false and I shall be broken-hearted.

I remain always your friend for life.

Mary

Dear Sol,
In a way it is hard for me to understand why you haven't written to me, a friend in the hospital. I have acclimated myself to this environment, although I feel knocked out all day. At night I am somewhat better. One of the other patients calls me a night blooming orchid. You know, Sol, it's nice writing you this way as a friend, but I'll be terribly hurt if you don't answer. I don't want pity, just a letter. I hope you are doing well at school.

Yours,
Mary

Dear Sol,
I wish I didn't love you so, then I wouldn't eat my heart out wishing, and wanting just a word from you, letting me know you haven't forgotten me. You said you'd write as a friend and I depended

on this. Now I know you must have been kidding. Once I didn't answer you and you told me it was rude and that silence was horrible to endure. I know what you mean. It makes it even harder to bear that I am lying on a hospital bed crying myself to sleep. How stupid of an intelligent girl of twenty-one, old enough to know better, crying over a man who doesn't love her anymore.

Be my friend. Please write. Now when I really need friends, I find I have none except my family. Why must I suffer so? I am pleading with you. Have you no mercy? I have made mistakes, but I am sorry, I've paid, oh, Sol, I love you so, please write. I am ill and unhappy and lonesome. Sure, I try to be cheerful. I keep everyone laughing, but inside it hurts. This is fate—I, Mary Castle, capable of having men fall at her feet, pleading with a man who turns his back when she needs him most. Please find it in your heart to write. Is this too much to ask?

Mary

Dear Sol,

Upon returning to my room this afternoon, I found a package from you. I was so excited that I could hardly open it. I am thrilled with the book and know I shall enjoy reading it. However, I must admit that I cried when I read your inscription. You see, I still had hopes of getting you back. I am fighting for your love. But those two lines: "In Remembrance Of Things Past, And Wishing They Could Last," made everything seem so final. I hope you didn't mean that things were completely over. When you left you said that I would have the chance to recapture your love, but those two lines inscribed in the book have sent me into a turmoil. You are all I need, want, or ever really loved in the whole world. Is everything over? Sol, be honest with me. I must know. I'm throwing myself at you but I must make clear how much I love you.

I shall always treasure the book. If you had sent me a card, or note, I would have loved it even more.

Mary

Dear Solon,

Your thoughtfulness in sending Mary a book was very much appreciated by her but the two lines inscribed upset her very much. She gathered that you were through with her. If this is true, please do not let her know through writing. If it is not so, please explain to Mary.

Also, the doctor remarked that if you should sign, "Love," in your letter, do so only if you really mean it. Otherwise, use some other form of closing, as Mary takes it literally. I will sincerely appreciate any delicacy you can display toward her.

It's not easy to "play the game," is it?

Thanking you,
Oliver Castle

Dear Solon,

I carry the letter you finally deigned to write in my purse in order to have this priceless document with me at all times. Whenever I am in need of communion with one of the great minds and spirits of our time, I haul it out and spell out every immortal word. It's unbelievable how many times I've parsed those metrical, measured, cheerful sentences about looking forward to summer and evincing an interest in us at home. Imagine evincing an interest in us at home. I find you truly extraordinary, one of the most unique human beings who ever lived, in the fantastic way you handle tragedy. Your technique of rendering tragedy harmless is, after all, quite marvelous, like Mr. Magoo, the old cartoon character who passes through earthquakes and cyclones without even knowing they are there much less having a hair on his head out of place. Meanwhile, not to worry, everybody here is suffering horribly and nobody is cheerful. I've just left the Castles who are, of course, suffering beyond measure. I wish I didn't admire Mr. Castle so much, but I do, and this makes me a part of his pain.

I don't know what to say to you about your letter. After Mr. Castle begged you not to be so cute, you finished off with your "truth" sermon. Is that what it means to become a lawyer, to insist on the "truth"? Is drowning in the bathtub truth? Don't worry, although I wish you would, and even pop a vessel or two, I haven't breathed a word of this kettle of carp to Mom or Pop. Mom keeps speaking of how badly you'll want a car when you come home. She's pleading with Pop. She worked on him an entire evening and has him partially convinced, although it would be a big expense. Mom asks if you can find a good buy up there that you could drive home. If you run into anything worthwhile, she says she'll swing it. You know they can't afford it, but don't let that bother you. It never did before.

Your sometime sister,
Phyllis

V

DAYS WHEN BIRDS COME BACK

These are the days when birds come back,
A very few, a bird or two,
To take a backward look.
                    —*Emily Dickinson*

A vision of himself, good or bad, had he ever had it? David Stein. Did the words conjure up a neat picture of a man, himself? It was not a matter of intelligence or, certainly, of introspection. Simply a point of view he had never been able to achieve. He just couldn't see himself. Whenever he tried, the idea would falter and crash blindly like a spent model airplane (not like the giant jetliner in which he was sitting, at least so far). In order to develop identity he had to rely upon social contact. Not for him the dreadful anomie of a single man in a boardinghouse. Friends and acquaintances snapped his picture, and all that he was he owed to others. And what is plaintiff's lawyer's, that is, David Stein's, reputation among his friends for truth, morality and chastity? Not as simple a question, Your Honor, as it first appears on a divorce blotter. It really depends on the witnesses. Some people, most, as a matter of fact, think that I have an excellent if somewhat shabbily coutured reputation, but then they don't know me too well—no one does, so they claim—and their opinion is suspect. Now if you were to permit my Caesar's wife Phyllis to take the stand—I realize that is impossible. I believe on the whole she likes me a little—but she finds me terribly ridiculous too of course. She scrutinizes a head too large and round for its square body and the bits of coal stuck into the snowman for eyes. Do you think she's off the mark? I don't. The nose and lips are thick. She considers him grotesque, I'm sure, albeit a gentle grotesque. If he weren't gentle, why on earth would she have married him? She knows that he is a serious man, serious about her welfare, willing to be taken for a clown so long as she is willing to admit, isn't she? that he isn't really a clown.

Then there is Aggie Crown, whom I've come to visit in New York. You know, my wife's beautiful college friend who visited us in St. Louis last month and with whom I became acquainted in what used to be, what still in obscure backwater pockets might be, the most desperate of circumstances. The circumstances? Well I can hardly divulge them because they would tend to compromise my present situation. You must realize that Aggie's attitude is likely to be ambiguous.

David glanced shyly at the young man sitting next to him. After their brief conversation following takeoff at St. Louis, the man had turned to the window or feigned sleep. What had he constructed from Stein's fleshy clumsiness? Why had this muscular tweed turned its unstuffed shoulder on David, tail-wagging sheepdog of a David, only too anxious to be a friend of startlingly luminous-eyed man? The ancient Hebrews hated dogs, and so did the Polish shtetl Jews, not without reason, was this unleavened bread being visited upon David, an ancient Hebrew of thirty-three, by a crew-cut blond boarhound who might be somewhere in his twenties but, with his looks, was forever ageless? The man met David's eyes and decided to manufacture a smile and David, to emphasize his diasporic goodwill, nodded vigorously, only to have the man turn his shoulder on him back to the window as if to say that David was overstepping his bounds, was being grossly familiar with his betters, and David wasn't at all, he indeed knew his place with others if not with himself, and hadn't invaded the other's privacy for over an hour. Here, at the moment before they would land at LaGuardia and undoubtedly never see each other again, all he hoped for was that when that tall, handsome stranger ripped David's portrait from his Polaroid he'd make the presentation of it an act of patronal kindness. But that was not to be. As the plane taxied to a stop and the passengers began to worry and tug at their carry-on luggage, David saw himself with blue, pellucid eyes as that bustling, vulgar prototype of Jews driven to madness by good manners denied them. And he was certainly not prepared for the deadly serious game he was selected to play with Aggie.

He saw her at the gate and almost immediately she flew at him, a long-legged silken beauty dressed by *Mademoiselle*: green-and-black tartan skirt, knit wool green stockings, and a soft gray car coat with raffish fur collar. She flung her arms around him and kissed him on his cheek. Who was he at that moment? What did Aggie and the people milling at the gate and the boarhound at his heels see? With the strangers it was easy: a wife, a young, curved, soft thing, having married (for money, why else?) must greet her circumcised yoke with flute-like cries as he returns from a business trip, must allay suspicions of passionate affairs with innumerable blond, blue-eyed lovers. As to Aggie, overcoming a natural repugnance naturally, she was reliving the moment last fall when they told her that she, their angel of mercy, could arrange the saving of their lives as naturally as breathing in her two-hundred-dollars-an-ounce perfume, or the moment later when they knew she was absurdly theatrical enough to save their lives. It was nothing more than this, the whole scene, David knew quite well, plus Aggie's natural (there went that word again, the word he so admired in others because it was so alien to himself) flair—but he also knew that there was no choice, at least for Phyllis and him, there had to be something more for them if there was to be anything at all. The enormity of the situation—what they expected of Aggie, what they, in their vulgarity and pushiness, demanded of her rare and exclusive beauty and what, in her almost goddess-like disregard of the rules of the game, she had agreed to—appalled him.

Aggie restored equilibrium simply by disengaging herself from David, and as though striking the proper balance, balancing social scales, snipping here and adding there, filling in east and excavating west, confounded David by throwing her arms around the boarhound following on David's heels from the plane, only this time her open lips sought open lips, tongues coyly deployed themselves in the dark caverns, and they stood there locked in the kind of embrace that baffled censorship, that knew it belonged to the world before rubber stamps. David stood by measuring the sad weight of his otherness. It was too appalling to consider that Aggie knew this fellow biblically who had already picked up David by the fleshy scruff and shaken him loose from a dignity he never had. A casual set partner and now a full-fledged, clear-eyed danger. But they were both coming at him now and the transparent eyes, the other end of blindness's seesaw, were surrounded with radiating ski-bum's wrinkles. He sees David Stein as a monstrous joke composed by devilishly pretty, don't you know? Aggie for his fugitive amusement: come now, Aggie old gel, this may be sporting for a chuckle or two at the airport, but why are you taking this, this person's arm and mine, linking us? Really. "This is simply marvellous. Absolutely and definitively incredible," said Aggie. "Imagine meeting my two men at the airport—not any two men mind you, but the two most wonderful men in the world."

You're Stein," said the boarhound. "I'm Raleigh Purvis. Aggie's told me about you. Even if I hadn't sat next to you on the plane, I'd know you." "How, Rolly, old boy? By the smell, of course." And David knew but no longer with a sinking feeling—there was something stubborn in David that brought him back time and again from the cutting edge, he was to the manor born for brinkmanship—that for Rolly nothing had changed and the tone in the voice was the same disdain of the eye made articulate. What are we going to do with you, Stein? How can you be made to understand that you don't belong? Of course David knew more than Rolly could ever know that he didn't belong, he would *never* belong, that he subliminally never *wanted* to belong, that nothing had really changed in the world's master plan for Jews among gentiles since gentlemen's agreements of past decades, just as nothing in the hard little nut of being would change for blacks among whites, just as nothing ever changed between cattlemen and sheepmen, or Judge Temple and Natty Bumppo. People, as Hobbes pointed out to anyone who would bother to listen, simply didn't like each other, unless they were mirror images of themselves.

"Then you already know each other?" said Aggie. "It's as small a world, then, as only a cliché can make it, isn't it, my two beautiful people." Rolly found this amusing enough to curl a lip, as blatant as a wink, at David. "One big happy family is what we are. Did you drive my car out?"

"Of course, Rolly. You know perfectly well that I'd do whatever you asked me to do."

"Sure you would." He looked at David. "Give you a lift somewhere? What's your hotel?"

"Don't be absurd," said Aggie quickly. "David will of course stay with me. With my mother and me. We have loads of room in the apartment. I wouldn't hear of anything else."

Rolly pursed his lips. "Is that so?" he said. "You'd do anything for good old Stein, right?"

"Of course. I wouldn't dream of letting my Abram go to a hotel." And David, unnerved once again by blue eyes, winced.

"Who or what the hell is Abram?" said Rolly.

And it was Aggie who finally winked. "Just my pet name for David, that's all."

"Christ," said Rolly. "Let's go, then, if Abram's ready. You ready, Abram? Ready for the Big Apple?"

"Lead on," said David grimly, as he reviewed himself as a blob of property, domesticated animal retrieved at the baggage counter, stroked by Aggie's milk-white designation of David and Phyllis as her "first and always, her chosen people, her Abram and Sara." Then it had seemed innocent enough, on their turf, in their kitchen, amidst the high jinks that defined the relationship between Phyllis and Aggie. Now in the polluted, high-octane, merciless air of LaGuardia it seemed ugly and, however unintended, malicious.

"Got any luggage?" pursued Rolly.

"No. This bag is all I brought."

"All? How long you planning to stay?"

"Just a few days," said David. He wanted to placate the outrage in the other man's voice, an outrage he shared, he wanted to say, Surely you don't believe that the Levite plans a fate worse than death for your beauteous friend, do you? Knowing nothing between you more than an egg-sucking kiss, not having found in letters to the editor one reference to a Raleigh Purvis, surely you shouldn't be drawing a frown about you like a shroud. If you are a baseball fan, Rolly, you'll remember it's not over till it's over.

And yet I, David Stein, sometime Abram, *do* intend that fate worse than death for your friend and I do know, how? don't ask me how or I'll give you more how than you ever imagined, that Aggie is your intended whatever she intends, although how far you intend is not yet clear. I examine your clearly carved nostrils and your clear blue eyes, and what you intend is as clear to me as the Internal Revenue Code's impenetrable allocation of expenses between taxable and nontaxable income. I shudder with you at the idea that you must, even for a moment, brush an uncomplicated elbow against my grubby tax-ridden mind or my soup-stained soul. But, dear Rolly, old chum, old pal, sharer of my dreams, I have no choice. My destiny lies not in myself but in the bosom of Aggie, out of Abram and Sara. Forgive me, Rolly, for they have informed me what I must do.

"A few days, hey, where the action is, right? You come to New York often? On law business, right?"

"Right," said David. "I'm a lawyer," and had to add, "I suppose you could call it business."

Rolly, no dummy then, immediately picked it up. "Christ, is that what they call a legalism?" David considered the other man's height. At least six four, head and shoulders over most men, certainly over David, a barely respectable five ten. Aggie, walking between them, stared straight ahead, intensely, abnormally quiet. What do you perceive, Aggie dear? No holds barred, not at this late stage of the game. On one hand, the tall, beautifully muscled attacker of wild boars rooting among the tangled skein of nerves and vertebrae, and on the other, the timid house pet, Abram, arching his jugular vein toward the sharpest teeth this side of the Hudson. Which shall you choose? Indeed more of a dilemma than you pictorialized back in St. Louie. For you must remember, your ordinary, basic synapses never quit, you must remember that the pet might, with weak eyes and trailing courage, fighting very special fights, might rescue you from very special dragons. Like Rolly. So that I, schizophrenetic David-Abram Stein, hemmed in by vastly superior forces, must pin my faith, like a medal of honor, on your whimsicality. You certainly do have a natural (there flies away that word) talent, darling Aggie, for reifying flights of fancy.

"All right, then. Right on," said David. "I'm here strictly on business."

"Too bad," said Rolly, "you couldn't bring the wife and kiddies and combine business with pleasure. And how do the little woman—what's her name, Phyllis?—and all the little Steins take to all these business trips? I bet they get to really miss the old man, huh?"

David hesitated and slanted his eyes toward the horizon before Aggie could sweep up and capture them. "There are no little Steins," he said. "But Phyllis is fine. She understands these things."

"Phyllis is fine. Too bad she couldn't come with you to visit her old college chum, isn't it? I know, she'd get in the way of the business. And of course she's tied up with that nasty business of housekeeping. A lousy job but somebody's got to do it, right?"

"Actually she is tied up. She's getting her Ph.D. in comparative literature and couldn't afford to miss classes." And David, ruefully, could not resist a remark that could only cause further trouble. "Besides, she had to stay home with the dog," he said. "We don't do kennels."

"Lovely, lovely Uriah," said Aggie, her suddenly reactivated voice tragic. "How is my sweet, adorable Uriah?"

"Oh, my God," said Rolly. "Sorry," not sorry at all. "Lots of people use dogs as surrogate kids. Not to worry." He deliberated, hot on the scent. "How long have you been married, Stein?"

"Three years."

"And no little Steins. What the hell you waiting for, if I may be so bold?" and with that they reached the car, a new, gleaming Buick. They all (David was aroused enough to insist on his natural rights with Aggie) jammed into the front seat with Aggie, of course, offering each a thigh, in the middle. You, Aggie, are in the middle, you must remember this and that a kiss is still a kiss, and that you must take sides, first one, then the other, then the ultimate and irrevocable one. Perfect crimes go awry on the unpredictable, the dropped eyeglass, the scrap of cloth, the strand of hair. You, Rolly, are my unpredictable and you threaten the equilibrium. You suspect me already, you shrewd, sarcastic hulk. You examine my clogged pores and know that I wouldn't dare to stay with Aggie (her mother, a lush, doesn't count) if some dark, deep, Levantine thing between us didn't give the right, and more. It was unalloyed disgust at first sight but a splash of blind hazel coats your crystal blues, you arhythmic before the new image, off-beats of vintage Peter Lorre, of a soft-voiced, soft-muscled capacity for evil. Your imbalances drive the car more swiftly than you should and Aggie, securely tongue-and-grooved between her two men, nevertheless is alarmed. "Rolly, for Heaven's sake, slow down. Why are you driving so fast? You'll get a ticket if you don't kill us first."

"So what. Our mouthpiece is with us, isn't he? Welcome, Mr. Abram Stein, to the New York courts. You did say you were on business or did I get it wrong?" Nevertheless, Rolly slowed down. Aggie, you play your ends well against your middle. Now it is David Abram's turn. Really, Aggie, you are no mean slouch in the hardball business, with a smooth athletic thigh pressed remorselessly against David's grossness. You want so much to convince him, or at least yourself, that he is tall, strong, blond, blue, because wishing has so many other times made it so. You shut your eyes so tightly that you see his metamorphosis in the stars, and then you can't stop crying because you don't want the tall, strong, blond-blue unless he isn't there, remains immaterial. Actually you trembled and bit your pillow (you *must* have) when Phyllis wrote that he was coming to New York and you wrote back that it would be wonderful (no, no, yes, yes) you were ready, you'd die for them, your life belongs to them because you've chosen them, you said so, but, cross your heart and hope to die, how much of it did you mean, or more pregnant, how much of it did you mean to mean?

But you cannot utter a word of any of this to Abram because Rolly has no pinstriped intention of not listening.

They glided along the highway. Silence paved the way, their own and that of the big city which, after all, stayed up till all hours to worry about late-night noises. Somewhere in St. Louis, perhaps, at one of the sleek new hotels like the Omni or the Adam's Mark, between television programs, they were talking about *really* watching television, along the gay white way, at the Plaza perhaps, or the Sherry Netherland, tuning in as it were on the insistent beat of life in living color—there they were, huddled about their knees, watching their own myth being performed and believing too in its reality. And Aggie, where had she gone to commit her awesome act of resurrection and the life? Had she perhaps traveled back along their uneasy track, for it was uneasy after all, what else could it be? and rather than make the scheduled pit stop, run over the remains of her light fantastic St. Louis self. And having ground it into an unpalatable pulp, swallowed it nevertheless, egested it nevertheless, and now, revived, had determined to make it and herself whole once again? In whom could she confide? Rolly, as he used to be before I had made him what he was? Would he understand, forgive? Should she simply chalk it off with the rest of her real-life fantasies? Somehow, David felt she couldn't do that and feel as special as the occasion demanded of her and as she demanded for herself. I know, Aggie, why you are quiet as carpet slippers and how can I blame you? You are sitting between your lives.

"Here we are," said Rolly and double-parked. The engine was so quiet that it might have been turned off but David could tell from Rolly's grip of the wheel, his stare down the dark street, that no such concession had been made. I tell you, Stein, that you are bumbling into an area where nothing grows that is not lovely to see and smell, where lush lives linger over delicate flowers and singing birds, where pearl ears listen to songs of songs. Stein, go home. Beauty can kill.

David got out and waited mutely at the open car door. Aggie, with a hand on Rolly's sleeve, said, "Come up for a drink, Rolly. Please. I want you to."

"I don't think so. I'll let you and Abram talk over the good old days."

"Please, Rolly."

Abruptly Rolly turned off the ignition. He shrugged and released the door locks. They walked into an apartment building and were met at the elevator by a sleepy-eyed operator who took them up. You, Abram, are to be impressed by the casualness of the double-park in a city that grinds double-parkers up and spits them out. And you are. You glance timidly at the tall young man who stands brooding away from Aggie, from you, and you want to reassure him about Aggie but you can't. You feel as helpless as any executioner.

As the elevator stopped, Rolly said, "Wait, please," to the operator and walked with them to the apartment door. Aggie fastened her hands on Rolly's lapels. "Rolly."

"I'll call you tomorrow. Don't worry, rain or shine, I'll call you." He turned to David. "See you around." He held out a hand and David, surprised, took it. It was a careful-of-the-bones shake which surprised and, even more, said don't smile back, we can do without hypocrisy around here, I haven't changed my ideas about you, but until I know what the fuck's going on, we can at least touch gloves. They watched him go. "Call me early. Promise," said Aggie and Rolly, moving away, nodded and waved.

It was a strong reunion for the college classmates, Aggie Crown and Phyllis Stein. Although they wrote and called and religiously kept alive their idea of best friendship, they hadn't seen each other for several years when Aggie came to St. Louis in a form-fitting brown wool dress showing off her nicely rounded breasts and belly. The girls threw their arms around each other and made woman-love full of tears while David watched patiently. Then Aggie tore herself away from Phyllis and came at David, giving him all of her curved self until David became anxious and Phyllis laughed with joy. Aggie next demanded "a drink and the proper music, you damn well know what I mean, Phyl, if you remember anything," and Phyllis said, "I certainly do," so she put on the Berlioz Requiem, and Aggie, with slow, professional undulations, removed her soft brown wool dress, her underthings, her shoes and silk stockings until she stood grandly nude, her lovely arms raised to point the way to pale half-moon breasts. Phyllis, showing the wicked gleam of her black eyes, which made David sweat even more, danced about on praying mantis legs until that familiarly lean, muscular body was bare to the bone, and the two women swayed before uncertain David daring him to speak or even think their language. So David, drawing from his meager reserves, stood up and dropped his trousers and the rest until the square, fleshy body he had disowned long ago was exposed to their delighted, cruel eyes. They rocked with college-day laughter, pointing their long, phallic fingers at him and he stared away from each his own fig leaf. They took his hands and ran him through the rooms, with a discomfited, decorous Uriah complaining at their flesh-covered heels, until they were so exhausted that they collapsed onto living room chairs, and Aggie couldn't wait to tell them her belly was round because she was three months gone with a bastard child, and she doubled over in gulps of laughter while her breasts swung free. "Imagine," she said, "Aggie Crown, the libertine, a bug in a bottle."

Oh pooh, barked Uriah, sniffing up Aggie's leg. Is that all this rumpus is about? As if dogs wear clothes, as if they didn't invent bitchiness. Another dizzy dame to worry about.

You hush, said Phyllis to Uriah. You think you know it all.

I do, growled Uriah. Motherhood is God's gift to women, instead of giving them something nice, like four legs. What's the fuss?

Your daddy's a lawyer, said Phyllis. Let him tell you. Haven't you heard of *flagrante delicto* or *bastardy* or, to put it in lawyer solipsisms, *illegitimacy*? A child born out of wedlock, my dear dog, simply won't do in the eyes of the law, and those awful, baleful juristic eyes will have it, won't they? every time.

I don't understand a word you're saying, said Uriah, but I'll defend to the death your right to say it. My credo is, all babies, even dog babies, cry at night.

Shut yourself up and go lie on your blanket at the fire, said Phyllis. Who asked you to butt in?

Uriah, in a huff, snarled a bit at Aggie, just to show her who the real boss was around there, condescended to give her furless leg a final sniff, and trotted to his blanket. Even in his pride he couldn't resist listening, and cocked an ear. He pretended to be asleep but didn't fool anybody.

"I tried to cut it out," said Aggie, "in New York. Look at my new scar." They looked at her belly, which was as unmarked as a pauper's grave, and Aggie whooped at the deception. "Do you really, I repeat, do you really think I might? I should have it, I should have it not," she recited, her finger at her lips. "Eventually I may want to kill myself. I'm an old-fashioned girl at heart, you know. What do you think?"

Uriah couldn't resist. Oh, come now, he said. You're all bark and no bite.

That dog, said Phyllis, David, if you don't do something. Put him in a closet. David went over and absently patted Uriah on the head. He scratched him behind an ear and Uriah looked devout.

"What about an abortion or is that too Victorian?" said Phyllis.

"I've done that," said Aggie in all the glory of her wide eyes and innocence. "Lord knows I've done that. It's such a bore."

"And conclusive right at the beginning," said Phyllis and they both found something to laugh at in that before Phyllis straightened up and said slowly, "What about having it after all and giving it to me. We could adopt it. I'm barren myself. Can't have any. Tried and tried. Can't have any."

"Good heavens," said Aggie. "You mean it, you actually want one? What on earth for?"

Phyllis grinned. "The thing to do is what you can't or haven't, isn't that what you've been saying all along? Boredom is like taxes, to be avoided at all cost."

"Well," said Aggie meditatively, "you know I'd do anything for you but you'd hate the father. An awful scab. Madison Avenue with three children and wet brown eyes. No insult intended, darling Uriah."

My eyes aren't wet, said Uriah. Perhaps a drop or two here and there just to wet the whistle. That's all. Much you know. If you think you're letting your nameless bastard onto my turf, you've got another thought coming. I knew the minute I laid my dry eyes on you, you bitch, you'd cause trouble.

Listen to him, said Aggie, and lay down on Uriah's blanket, cuddling him against her repulsively blanched belly. I could go for you, Uriah, in a big, big way, she said. Uriah wriggled free and stared dryly. What crap. Let's set the record straight. I hate your whiteness, your smoothness, and above all your unnatural, unpelted, *shaved* look, as though a vet has done a job on you. No wonder you have to wear Dior clothes.

Aggie, despite the abuse, lay on Uriah's blanket and refused to give it back to him. Suddenly, she stopped smiling at Uriah and appraised David instead, and then her eyes caught and held Phyllis's. Phyllis seemed hypnotized. "Why not, Phyl?" said Aggie. "What about it? You game? David's adorable. He'd make a wonderful father."

"Yes, I truly think he would. And he's a lawyer. And that would make it legal," breathed Phyllis. They both centered upon David who grew uneasy and hugged his thighs with his arms. "Relax, David," said Phyllis. "This is Eden. Have a wonderful time and don't look over your shoulder. Aggie's making you an offer you simply can't refuse.

"What offer?" asked David stupid with old-fashionedness.

"She'll get her abortion and then Aggie and you can have our child. It's a once-in-a-lifetime offer and, I repeat, it's one you can't refuse."

"I can't refuse," said David slowly.

"That's right, David," and Phyllis grinned at Aggie. "I really think he's got it."

"I really think he does," said Aggie. "Then it's settled. Now let's see about a timetable. I do need a little time to straighten out my affairs in New York. Overdue library books and such. Things do have a habit of piling up. So, okay. I'll write you when I'm ready, okay? But it's definitely a go situation, my darlings, my chosen ones, my," she concluded inspiredly, "Abram and Sara." She laughed, hugged Phyllis, hugged David and instructed him. "Don't look so worried, David. I'm quite good at this sort of thing. Trust me. Absolutely nothing can go wrong."

"You can manage it, David," said Phyllis. "Another I, another you, it's all the same. And you can't deny it's for a worthy cause."

"No," said David. "I can't deny that."

Yes you can, said Uriah almost weeping. Say it's against man and nature. And you a lawyer. Why is it any better than buggery and you won't allow that. Be a man, David. Stand up for man's rights, for God's sake. Are you a man or a mouse? Whatever they say about dogs, they wouldn't ever let themselves be a mouse. So at least be a dog if you can't be a man.

Shut up, dog, and don't make me say it again, said Phyllis. One more male chauvinistic piggish crack out of you and I'll lace you with Tylenol. You want trouble, I'll dog you the rest of your miserable life. And bold Uriah curled up with a whimper. Okay already, he said, you can all go to hell in a basket as far as I'm concerned.

"Look at it this way," said Phyllis. "Aggie prefers suicide to boredom, you heard her, and suicide is, after all, a high-water mark of morality. Don't be fooled by Aggie's pretty face. She'd love to commit suicide. I know her because I knew her when. She's read too many good books."

"High camp aside," said David, finally daring to lay cards on the table and look Phyllis steadily in the eye, "is this what you really want?"

Phyllis, surprised, hesitated, then nodded and said gravely, spacing her words, "Of course I mean it. I wouldn't say so if I didn't mean it. You know that I mean it or you don't know me at all. And it's not high camp at all. It's more like the enemy camp if you'd only bother to stop and think about it."

"All right then," said David, and struggled to say something, anything, that would make his body, if only for a little while, come back to him and make him whole, make him invulnerable to civil wars. It was, of course, a hopeless yearning. His body and he had been estranged for much too long. He could only murmur beyond their hearing, so that only Uriah could make out the sounds.

And in a blink, Aggie was back with them flat-bellied and beautiful. And, after a drink or two, she began to take off her clothes again, rehearsing the litany of "my special people, my chosen people, my Abram and Sara" until it found absurd echoes in David's troubled heart.

By the time Aggie entered the bedroom, David was prepared. He had changed into his best pajamas and washed his best face and brushed his best teeth. His face in the strange mirror looked terribly grotesque: fleshy and misshapen. He pinched his middle and wondered what pinprick would bring reality. None of the facts of the situation, none of them seemed quite as incredible as the idea that Aggie's beautiful body was to submit to his. He refused any longer to acknowledge that his was the more likely submission and that Aggie had never surrendered to anyone in her life, nor was ever likely to. It was the point in riverboat drama at which the blond hero bounded center stage and, felling the mustache-twirling villain, dark as any sea-dingle, caught the swooning lady, clothed in curls and dimples, in his arms. The cast was present even unto as orthodox a hero as one could want, Raleigh Purvis, who must surely have doubled back and was now waiting for the ideally dramatic moment to burst through the door.

Instead, with the softest of knocks, to perpetuate the pretense that Aggie maintained about her mother's duenna-ship, this same mother who had been drunk from the moment David met her and who was now undoubtedly snoring in her bed, Aggie entered, dressed in a white lace nightgown that, unlike her nakedness David remembered from St. Louis, denied nothing, promised all, left everything of her loveliness to the imagination, that said as emphatically as a bowling strike, David, see it, do you see it? No pins of reality here. Not a cough in a carload or a trout in the milk here. We are gathered, beloved, in the sightlessness of us all and do you, decoded and declassified essence of David, take this woman? and do you, curved lip of Cupid's bow, take this, this . . . aposiopesis? With ritualistic purity she smiled at him sitting in the chair, slipped out of her gown and into his bed, covering up to the chin. He stood up and over her, man in all his red meat and silver oysters, beat his chest and yodeled: it was operation child.

Trembling, he got into bed beside her and they lay silently, both on their backs, their sides barely touching. David had time, suddenly a great deal of time that hung like a bundling board between them, to wonder where all sense of sex had gone. He reached out for remembrances of eroticism he had practiced or read about but his mind was seething with time, with seconds, minutes, hours, days, months, years, he went free-falling through thousands of years of past until those years became seconds of future, then minutes, hours and he was living, no, reliving because he had spent many futures here already, many more thousands of years than the world had left. He whispered to himself, without even Uriah there to hear him, and yet this is the beautiful Aggie Crown, and why can't I take her with me?

"What are you thinking?" she said.

He cleared his throat. "Only that this is the beautiful Aggie Crown in bed with frog-prince David."

She turned toward him, and the pressure of her body became firm, to let him know with no ifs and buts that she was of the here and now, make no mistake about that. "So you think I'm beautiful?"

"I do," he said, and because the words were so ceremonious, he felt betrayed by himself and asked, "Who is Raleigh Purvis?" With a slight shiver she rolled away and broke contact. "Just a lad. We went to high school together. A mere infant my own age who fancies, only fancies, mind you, that he's in love with me. But he is cute, don't you think?"

David was astonished to learn that Rolly, the baby, was only two years younger than hoary David. "And you, what about you?"

"What about me?"

"What do *you* fancy?"

She laughed. "Men," she said. "I fancy men. But he is cute, isn't he?"

"Very," said David. He was drenched with the image of the big strong body, the close-cropped hair, the fiercely blue eyes, all of it hurting at the alien intrusion, unable to fight weakness.

"He's in the investment banking business, something of the sort.

That's why he was on the plane, a convention in San Francisco. Actually he wanted to be a doctor but couldn't get into med school, and it upset him terribly because his father and brother are doctors. So you mustn't judge him too harshly."

"I, judge him?" said David in astonishment and some anguish at being so misunderstood. "I wouldn't dream of it, please believe me. What right would I have to judge him?"

"Every right," said Aggie swiftly. "Every right in the world."

"I think he's very nice," said David stubbornly. "I like him. I think if I knew him better I would like him very much."

"He is very nice," said Aggie and sighed. "If only he weren't such a child." They lay in silence side by side, robots on parallel assembly lines, not touching until Aggie, convulsively, rolled over and pressed her soft length against him. She rested her hand on his stomach and it was really the first moment that David understood she was prepared to fulfill her natal vows. She intended to have his child, a fantastic surmise, for reasons which didn't exist, at least on his earth. And him, what was his reason? He had to search the barren waste of caked inner self for clues. There had to be more than the naked desire to honor Phyllis. Did he want a child that badly or at all for himself? He had no ready answer but he could distinguish the hazy outline of a good father in himself in days yet unborn. A good father of anybody's child, his own and not Phyllis's, or Phyllis's and not his own. For that matter, Aggie's and Rolly's.

What could Phyllis make of such a child? When she looked at the father what images of Aggie Crown? It was a sleep-flying scene, with no mirrors for reflection. The desire to please—only that? He wanted suddenly to leap from the bed and imperiously order Aggie from the room, her room. Would she laugh at him until her throat closed on the absurdity of him all? And what would Phyllis make of it, what agonies would she endure on top of those as she thought matters stood? And what would its ultimate impact be on Aggie, having offered and been refused, as if she were something on a department store counter to be cavalierly handled, squeezed for content, bent and twisted for flexibility, and then replaced, scarred and bruised, on display but probably good for nothing better than recycling? She might very well be in love with Rolly at the dark, weighted core of her lightness of being. He really couldn't tell. She was in the final analysis a hard read, and the present madness could be that final sowing of wild-oat promises before settling down to a life of love, honor, and obey. She was still some diminished, diluted kind of Catholic. Perhaps this was a diminished, diluted kind of penance for killing other children, nipping them as it were in the bud.

David saw clearly, clearer than he had ever seen in his life, perhaps more than would ever again be possible for him. He couldn't go through with it. But all the while her fingers were playing lightly all over his body and he had placed his hand upon her breast and could not will its removal.

What would be left of his marriage, what? Child or no child, intercourse or no, what? What would, what possibly could, Phyllis say or do with him when he returned? She could not have really expected him to go, at the very moment she would not take no for an answer, flooded him with her desire and made him love her as never before, she could not, any more than he, have really expected Aggie to keep her pledge, none of them could have expected the others to perform (is that how wars really started?) and here they were, businesslike arms around each other, kissing with the genuine passion born of myth, bodies moving in preterhuman rhythm, he could think clearly all night and it wouldn't do any good. Moral dialectic, dull as lead, might do as a shield from uranium but not from body heat; it melted away above a certain temperature. He realized that whatever he thought, it wouldn't concern this body no longer his, as if it ever had been, moving with its own soul. He could only sit idly by and let it live out its programmed life. What if, what if—David tried to summon up whatever he had in reserve and had never before learned to use, but it was hopeless. He was sitting on the chair beside Aggie and David thrashing on the bed, off on a long oceanic voyeurism, waiting for the inevitable closeout of gasp and wheeze, or if not that, at least a proper directive. Becoming a lawyer was a part of the scenario: a teacher of political science had pointed a long, bony finger and so he had gone to law school. A lucky choice, or so he had believed until now, because a lawyer's choices were dictated. A client would make a demand and he had merely to comply. David had to perform because that was the name of the game in a service industry. Lawsuits suited him and he suited lawsuits. They were each inert until moved—he had never been saddened and chastised by the realization until this moment as the bodies continued to thrash on the bed. Never before had he realized that inevitably even he must suffer through lack of will, that if he wouldn't be master of his fate, he could, and must, be captain of his moral choices, that if he loved Phyllis and honored Aggie's forbearance, he must let them know that like those millions of Ibsenian women, he chose love over honor. But how was he to let them know, if his body obeyed the echoes and not the essences of personality? Phyllis, and the thought, an unguided missile, staggered him, Phyllis didn't want a child so much as she wanted *his* child and that made all the difference.

He left the chair not without effort and joined his body on the bed, entering from the bottom where it was less heated, and it immediately shrugged away from Aggie and lay still. He was wet with perspiration and he could hear Aggie drawing gulps of air. He realized that she was crying and he reached carefully, making sure he touched only her hand. "Aggie," he said. "You are magnificent, truly. It's not you, of course. You know that, of course. I couldn't."

She buried her wet face in his neck. "Of course you couldn't, David. Of course you couldn't. I'm not crying for that. It's because I could, I really could, because it had a very good reason and I have very few reasons."

"There's Rolly," said David. "He might be a reason."

"He might, but he isn't," said Aggie. "He might have been but he couldn't be, not anymore." And David, amidst sorrow and skepticism (who was he compared to Raleigh?) was startled by the keenness of his pleasure that he was considered in some circles a preferential male. He thought about it and decided that he didn't feel guilty or sneaking about his en passant joy. The sensation was too new and too important. They lay quietly until Aggie slid out of bed. "I'll see you in the morning. Good night, dear Abram," she said and was gone, and David lay awake for hours, hoarding his ebullience, marveling at himself. Finally, he remembered that he was still in New York and determined to fly back the next day, on the early afternoon flight.

VI

FUN AND GAME DAYS

From the shore the lake resembled a stretch of iridescent gray cloth being played with by wind and dappled with round crests of black. On the near horizon the hills dipped and swelled, rough and green, and in the distance they turned black and stood like a ragged hemline. The waves made their pushes toward shore in gushes of exhalation, giant lungs breathing out as they came in. Solon Pepper, dressed in shorts and a zippered windbreaker, stood at the edge on the small pale rocks washed clean and yearned for the remembered romance of it. Once holding out his arms and screaming his dominium over sky and water, he could do crazy dances and drench himself with the promise of the future. He could fling himself in and out and lie panting in the sun and chant, you're great, Solon, you're wonderful. Solon wrapped the windbreaker around his chin and went inside the cabin.

It was early morning and methodically he set about the business of preparing for the day. Voluntary primitivism no longer gave him any pleasure. He lifted the iron disks from the top of of the Kalamazoo stove and stuffed in paper and log chunks, smiling as he poured on kerosene designed for the lamps. Even here one cheated on nature. The fire flared up ominously and he replaced the disks. Out on the porch he tilted forward the great, nearly empty water jar in its open-sided wood crate, removed the cork, and let water pour into the teapot for instant coffee.

The walk down the road to refill the jar led past Aggie Crown's cabin. There was no sign of her or her mother. Again he smiled. It amused him to think of the two elegant women going to their outhouse although the idea was no longer as funny as when, tiring of his summer in New York, getting his friend, Waller, to handle his case load for a week, he invited Aggie to go with him to Maine, and Aggie, unpredictable as ever, and as perverse, must bring along her mother.

The lake, the hills, the cabins, had not changed very much in four years, from when he had discovered them, his second year at law school, what he called the year of the great lump, which had turned out to be banally benign. Solon had changed a great deal. He had grown entirely used to life, and not even discomfort could change that. His return to Moosehead Lake was a snatching at a benign remembrance of things past. In a spasm of hedging he had thrown Aggie into the bargain. He had laid her on a blanket of pine needles under the giraffe-necked pines at the point, naked under a full-dress parade of Big and Little Dippers, and she had laughed and scratched her nose, and he mourned the betrayal of youth, his. She, his "older" woman, had the infuriating knack of making him feel septuagenarian.

His smile lingered as he passed the big house on the way to the water faucet connected to the spring. Billy, the seventeen-year-old son of the owner of the camps, was in love with Aggie, unable to keep his round eyes off her. Solon tried to construct Aggie as a pure stranger just met (through his sister Phyllis, actually), and her slim, perfect body with its high breasts, her oval wide-eyed face swept by fine loose hair, filmed his mind's eyes. It was no use. He could never gain Billy's vision, never had it, and his own was threadbare with its elbows showing. She was one of the riding habits that somehow moved him through the indistinguishable days and nights.

Solon set down the jar under the faucet and turned the water on. It trickled under the low pressure into the narrow mouth and Solon, waiting, looked down toward the public dock. A small wiry man was leaning over the outboard motor on the boat, filling it with gasoline. Now he stopped and swung a whisky bottle to his lips. None of them, it seemed, could do it quite alone. Sure, the man had told them at the office, it's off for two weeks of peace and quiet. Me and the boat and the fish and the big open lake and sky. Only now, once there, he couldn't go it without his ample supply of J. W. Dant.

The jar overflowed and water slopped on the ground. Solon turned the faucet handle in the wrong direction, forcing it tight against the screw, wasting more water. He reversed the direction and turned the water off. It pleased him to waste water here when it was so hard to come by at his cabin. With the jar heavy on his shoulder he started back. Aggie's cabin was still quiet. He imagined the women in their beds. The mattresses were old and soft and hollowed in the middle. Aggie would lie carelessly, limbs strewn about, breasts at half-mast, and her mother's worn-smooth flesh would be folded into the dips and swells, yielding to the softness with greater softness. Mrs. Crown was still not being counted out, despite her age and being a lush. It took a long time in certain special genetic cases for sex to go to seed.

It had been irritating to learn that she was coming along with Aggie but now he was almost glad because he had never expected Aggie, intoxicated by the crystalline Maine air, to become a clown. Aggie, undiluted, was getting harder and harder to take.

He swung the jar down to the porch table and rubbed his bruised shoulder. The sense of being alive occurred to him while rubbing and he stared at his broad chest and flat stomach. He sat in the wicker chair and, sliding on his spine, contemplated his heavily muscled, well-proportioned but infuriatingly short legs. They, and they alone, made him too short. For years during his early twenties when the future was still something to be guarded, something to be gift-wrapped in self-deception, he claimed to be five feet ten. Now at twenty-seven he called softly to the lake, "Hello there. I'm exactly five feet seven and three-quarters and who are you?"

The lake was restless. The waves slapped the shore as though it had gotten too familiar, and wind, ruffling the pages of his book lying forgotten on the table, beat at his face and reminded him to check the pilot light on the refrigerator. Picking up his old, moth-eaten woolen blanket lying in a heap at the base of the refrigerator and squatting on his haunches, huddling under the blanket, he opened the lower door. The light was out again.

He ignited the butane gas with his cigarette lighter, holding down the button until the click got things going again, and stood up, conscious of the ache in his legs. Life again through pain. How much pain, he wondered, could one trust before it ceased to represent life and merely parodied it? Grimacing at the fleshiness, he pinched his underarm hard and flexed his muscle until the bulge pulled his arm into shape.

Solon went into the cabin, made instant coffee, and took his cup to the straight-backed, armless wooden chair at the table. After a moment he placed the cup on the red-checkered oilcloth and lit a cigarette. In the morning the cabin was twilight gray and all of the wooden objects seemed hard and foreign. He rapped his knuckles on the table. "Come in, wood, and set awhile." His watch said nine o'clock. It was nice to be served breakfast by Aggie and her mother but they were getting up later and later and he wondered if he was getting tired of them. Surely not they of him, not Aggie as long as there were teases to test on him. Perhaps her mother but she seemed such a willing, anxious creature. Her husband, Aggie's father, had been dead for many years and left them extravagantly well off. Well, thank God, he no longer needed to give anybody's money more than a passing thought.

He went to the refrigerator and broke off some cheddar, wrapped stale bread around it and stuffed it into his mouth, then bent down and checked the pilot light. It was out again. He kicked the door shut. The hell with it, and walked out in front of the cabin at the shore to watch the waves kicking in, pick up and throw a handful of flat, smooth pebbles. The wind battered his face. He turned and walked up the pine-needle path toward the point. Just before the end, the path widened into a rough circle and he stood on it, eyes streaming from the wind, imagining himself and Aggie undulating under his feet. His heel, as though putting out a cigarette, twisted into the pine needles and gracefully they gave ground. Solon looked up at the pines, ragged with a partial shedding of bark, and noting one silver-smooth among rougher brothers, ran his hand along the trunk. He cursed as he got a splinter and pulled it out with his teeth. He decided to make another pass at Aggie's cabin and see if they were awake.

At her cabin there was still no sign of life. Solon kicked at pinecones and walked past toward the big house to check for mail.

Billy was sitting at the desk in the living room. He was a gangly kid with strong, irregular features and tawny hair. Solon, without bothering to smile, said, "Any letters?"

"Right here, Mr. Pepper," said Billy. He handed one letter over and Solon elected to say, "Thank you." He turned abruptly and walked out. It was appropriate, he felt, to try to keep the kid ill at ease if only because he was so self-possessed and on top of his tiny game in the backlands. Just let him come to the big city and see how much good his hunt-and-fishery would do him. The letter was from his sister Phyllis, and Solon stared coldly at the envelope, noticing without curiosity the St. Louis postmark, the bold, black, athletic, familiar scrawl. The envelope told him all he wanted to know, that she was alive, at least two days ago. The whereas and wherefores could be safely left to his shaggy-dog lawyer brother-in-law. He ripped the envelope open.

"Dear Solon," it went. "I have the most staggering news so don't think I'm needlessly violating your viciously precious privacy. Before that, however, I think it's wonderful that Aggie's up there to teach you some of the facts of life you can't seem to get through your semi-permeable membrane of a head. It's always seemed to me that if anyone could she could handle your particular brand of macho idiocy. That's what you need, for all our sakes, for a woman to put her brand on you, not, mind you, to capture you, no woman would be that ridiculous or god-forsaken, but simply to burn some flesh, raise some smoke from that impenetrable hide of yours. All of which is to say, I expect Aggie and you are having some memorable times together, you little hound dog you.

"I sound treacly and sentimental, don't I? Well, I feel that way. I'm no longer just another of the cynical, disillusioned Peppers and figure it's time I behaved more like Mrs. David Stein, woman released from liberation. Get ready for the big one, the Big Bang. I'm pregnant. Me, Phyllis Stein, hard-nosed Phyllis the first, candidate at thirty-one for mums of the year, isn't that the living end—or beginning? I love it, every precious palpitation and hot flash of it, and after you reflect upon it avuncularly and think of those incredibly expensive designer clothes for infants you're going to buy, you'll love it too. You've got to, or, chum, there's nothing out there for you, you may as well cash it in. A pregnancy is all that stands between us, you and me, and hydrogen bomb fallout, radioactive milk, acid rain, dioxin, and the rest. Think of it, Solon, if you can be an uncle and I can be a mother, then all is not lost, the unconquerable will, etc., etc.

"I'm writing Aggie too, so it isn't any secret for her not to know. I don't mind if it's emblazoned across the sky. I'm happy, dammit. Drink up, mates, Phyllis Stein is having a human baby. Forgive me, Solon, I know what the idea of anyone being happy does to your central nervous system. Try to love us (*it* at least), as I shall try to love you, and be happy for us, or at least try. Is it still conceptually possible? I hope so. I do. Phyl."

Solon's feet crunched pinecones. He had walked past Aggie's cabin without seeing it and didn't know whether they were up yet. At his own camp, he sat at the hole in the outhouse and stared at the letter, then at the low, tar-paper roof. In the corners spiders were hooking their webs and he resolved that this time he must remember to get a broom and sweep the invaders out. In an outhouse a man should be left alone, safe from needles, to read letters from his sister. It hadn't been so long ago (five years?) that she had fled her husband and ivy-covered house in the Midwest, had come to him while he was still at law school, to little Solon for succor. She was grieved to the quick at her marriage, wondering whether she should go on, and it was to Solon she turned for resolution. He had resolved it all right. She'd gone back to David and now had burned all other bridges behind her. It was a shock certainly. He had had an *idée fixe* that they (Phyllis and himself) wouldn't have children and it had been comforting to be frozen in their positions because it made noumena of progeny, too true to be real. With a child, he recognized immediately, she was lost to him.

And yet it hadn't been entirely his fault that he had offered her so little. She had come when he thought he was dying of cancer. The lump in his throat had been removed a month later and proved to be benign, but then it had filled his being and he had no room for other people. And after that there was the stupid, bloody business with Mary Castle. Solon got to his feet impatiently and left the outhouse. Even alone he spun dirty webs in outhouses. Even alone he was a liar. The truth was that he was bored, a crime in itself and certainly not an extenuating circumstance. He was manning a peephole, watching poker-faced, without bothering to believe another's crisis could be other than stagy, other than just not enough Valium. Solon opened a fist wide and closed it again, groping vainly for his sister, testing her joy.

He returned to Aggie's and this time they were up. The smells of bacon and eggs and coffee crowding through the clean morning air made him heady. He knocked once at the door and pushed it open without waiting. Aggie was standing at the stove in blue jeans and a gray lamb's wool sweater and Mrs. Crown sat at the table in a bright blue robe, sipping coffee. Aggie's round buttocks swelling tightly against the faded blue, and her mother's round breasts pushing loosely against her robe, combined in his mind with hunger and he wanted to cram them and the bacon and eggs all into his mouth at once until his scarred throat ached. Mrs. Crown smiled around troubled eyes and lifted her cup. "Coffee?" she said.

Solon poured coffee from the pot on the stove. He leaned over the pot and, sniffing with open mouth, tried Aggie's thigh with his own.

She did not move away and he swung around for a kiss. Instead she turned her face toward Mrs. Crown. "Mother, get the bread and butter out, would you?" she said, and when her mother went to the porch, Aggie smiled radiantly at Solon and goosed him with a fork handle. He jumped and half raised his arm to strike her. She laughed. "God, you goose well," she said. "In fact, you're the best goose I know."

"I've told you not to do that," he said, fighting to appear unruffled or he would have no chance at all, all the time not caring what the chance was. It was, as usual, hopeless. His anger glistened on his face. "I hate it. Can't you understand? I hate it."

Her smoky, web-fine hair swung across her face and into his eyes before she tossed it back. "All right," she said smiling into his eyes. "You hate it. You can kiss me with your hate-clenched teeth."

His anger rattled harmlessly against her tinny laughter and he marveled at the perfection of her face. Her beauty belonged to still life and everything she did to it depressed him. She gave it away in frivolity and he wanted to shake her. He would have been content to tie her into a chair and gag her mouth without asking for ransom. Passivity was all that became a beautiful woman, and Aggie was a girl on the go. He kissed her with his hate-clenched teeth. She pulled away and staring at him gravely tickled his armpit. He dropped to the bench at the table. The hell with her. The woods were full of sweet, compliant nymphs. Perhaps he could find one who'd thumb her nose at this one. For now there was breakfast.

And in a moment, while Mrs. Crown flapped in her mules toward the table with a loaf of bread and stick of butter, Aggie slid her white arms around his neck and kissed the back of his head. Her breasts were warm against his back. "Such a hate," she whispered, as sweet as any wood nymph. "You'll get yours later."

Mrs. Crown sat on the opposite bench and lit a cigarette. Her flesh was of the softness that, being pressed, preserved marks. Her cheeks and temples were crowded with wrinkles like the track of tiny insects. She must, once, have been as pretty as Aggie. Had she too, in the goodness of her time, goosed men, pushed them into lakes, put sand in their shoes? She appeared more deferential, more biblical, than that. A man, even Solon, seemed precious to her and to be treated with delicacy and not a little fear. He looked at the folds of her robe where they fell from her throat and had a fierce desire to rip them away. He raised his eyes to hers and was incredibly nervous. She was large, deep and hungry. He searched through his commonplace arsenal for familiar weapons of intellectual distance and mockery and found nothing but funny-house mirrors of her softness. This woman, he thought, is, deserves to be, somebody's mother-sweetheart.

Aggie put his plate of bacon and eggs in front of him and sat so that their legs made solid contact. Her hand stroked his thigh toward his center, she knowing full well how annoying it would be at breakfast. Bitterly he buttered a piece of rye and filled his mouth. Without her navigating fingers, he would have loved the sensation of eggs, bacon, bread and butter churning all together and on top of it the sober, serious taste of hot black coffee.

She was riding him too hard. Before Moosehead he had conceived of her as his sister's friend, giddy, beautiful, and lascivious, positioned nicely older than he, something nice for the Maine woods. The thing he had most counted on was her predictability and it was the one thing he could no longer count on. She was making sport of him. They were swinging on parallel bars and she tickled him to make him fall even when she thrashed under him on the pinecones. It had not before occurred to him that sex might be a form of athleticism even as much (which *had* occurred to him) as an intellectual exercise. He had often, from a telescoped distance, while lusting in dead seriousness after every minute of it, defined sexual passion as loose-lipped, biodegradable, top-dogged, but never had he termed it fun and games. She teased him, tripped him, tickled him.

He kept examining his shoes, prepared to find a matchstick burning down to the leather. At night he expected the bed sheets to be tied into knots. Yet every evening they went out to the point and he laid her on the pinecones. Nightly they performed the act of love and in her persistent refusal to treat it or him seriously he wondered with some anxiety if this was her form of being serious about the relationship. He speculated, and was annoyed at the spasm of pleasure it gave him, whether she could possibly be in love with him. Perhaps her definition of love was the infinite capacity of giving and taking pains.

After breakfast Aggie and he went for a walk and Mrs. Crown went back to bed. Once they were safely out of sight, Mrs. Crown would lie on her back, her robe loosened in inattention. She would stare, deep brown eyes glazed and lips parted, at the peeled log roof and then she would reach for the bottom drawer of the bureau and pull out her bottle of rye. When they got back to the cabin, she would be snoring gently, exuding rich, sweet odors of whisky, and Aggie would grin as though her mother had performed a miracle of humor and was ready for canonization.

As soon as they were on the path threading through the pines toward the marshy part of the lake, in the most private part of the woods, Aggie spun around and locked him to her with arms around his neck. As he stood, forgetful, soaking in the curves and planes of her breasts and stomach and thighs, one of her arms slid lingeringly along his chest. He closed his eyes in the profound attention of a dog being scratched on the rump, and she pinched his scrotum sharply, catching loose skin between the blades of two fingers. He pushed her away, attacked her breastbone with the heels of his hands, and she stumbled backward, tripped over a fallen log, and sat down across it. He was immediately contrite and rushed to help her up. She took his hand. "Damn it, Aggie, are you all right?" he said.

"Of course," she said, but was rubbing a skinned elbow which was beginning to sport dots of blood. Solon pulled out his handkerchief and dabbed at the elbow. He was genuinely alarmed because he saw her suddenly, for the first time, with a small feminine face puckered and ready to cry. He realized, in terms of masculine reserves, how defenseless she was and he was frightened. Had he become responsible for her? Was she *that* clever and devious and had she with a series of booby traps couched as practical jokes gulled him? He looked at her lovely oval face trembling with the determination not to weep and touched her elbow. "Aggie," he said. "Listen to me. Let's sit down a moment."

She turned away and he could see tracings of the rough, corrugated tree bark on her blue jeans. It reminded him of Mrs. Crown's face wrinkles and he was impatient that he could never be free, that each sensation led him to memory and memory to generalization and, finally, nothing was left but empty husks of emotions, things related rather than felt. "I'd rather not," she said. "I haven't much time. Billy's taking me out fishing in his boat."

"Billy," said Solon. "What on earth for? You've never fished in your life. You said you hated the thought of obsessive hooks in living flesh. When did this come up?"

"He invited you too if you care to go." She still hadn't turned and from the rear, holding her elbow, she seemed fragile and vulnerable, a nude porcelain figurine bent over itself in an abandoned museum. He was able to see himself as her vandal. For his taking her, what did she have a right to expect? Was it enough that with no witnesses other than, occasionally, her mother, she tweaked his nose and salted his coffee? He had accepted as her objective in going to bed, his own as well, the desire to be treated as object. Objects had no purpose and could strike each other, glance off without causing pain, and without reflection never meet again. Now, viewing her tangentially, she was entirely human and he didn't want to cause her pain. He never intended to cause pain. His malady, which he never thought about, was thoughtlessness, not malice. He suspected that for all her playfulness she wasn't having very much fun.

"I'd be a drag. By the way, the fish don't suffer at all actually. Their mouths are like the loose flesh on a dog's neck."

She turned to face him at this and he was stimulated by her laugh. It was probably the first spontaneous amusement he'd ever given her. "You sound properly professional," she said. "Come along with us."

"No thank you," he said. He hesitated. "Billy and I don't see eye to eye. He might push me off the boat. I've been treating him like a dopey kid and he resents it."

"He is a dopey kid," said Aggie. "Here's your chance to put him in his place, make a man out of him."

Solon shook his head. They were walking back down the path toward Aggie's cabin, and he was far from convinced that Aggie wasn't still playing him for a sucker, letting out his line so that she could bring him up short. "It's too late in the game for me with people like Billy, especially on his turf. I'm making a goal-line stand and have to conserve my energy."

"What on earth are you talking about? A stand against what? What game are you playing with soft, round Mother Nature that takes so much effort?"

"You've noticed my effort?"

"That you take Mother Earth so seriously? That you think life is a bowl of cherry pits? Of course I've noticed. What else is there to notice?"

Solon said slowly, "I suppose I'm pretty much an open book composed of Greek grave." They were at the cabin. He stopped and said, "Could you honestly, perhaps in extremis, say you like me?"

She leaned toward him and laid her cheek against his. "I can honestly say I could, if you weren't you and I wasn't me," she said wistfully, then laughed. "Or if I were the only girl in the world and you were the only boy." She went in. He stood at the door and remembered that his sister was having a baby and wondered, without enough interest to ask her, what Aggie's reaction was. He had always viewed the relationship between the two women with irritated amusement. Whenever they were together they charged each other with an excitement that excluded anybody else. It was as though they had gone through a war together, saved each other's lives, nursed each other's wounds. They were bosom buddies with a vengeance and he who had never had a buddy was repelled and fascinated by the wanton displays of affection. It confused him to witness what was generally regarded as the most precious and desirable of human qualities poured out as though it were inexhaustible. If it was so important to them, they should keep it in a perfume bottle and touch a drop behind each ear as it became necessary. With even prodigious penury, who could store up enough love for a lifetime?

He walked back to his cabin. The day loomed empty without Aggie. He had gotten used to her and the projects that might otherwise have satisfied him seemed tasteless. He sat on the porch and stared at the lake and invited the wind to buffet his face while he projected activities. The dishes would be washed, the floor swept, and if the water was warm enough, a swim would be taken. He would sit on the porch and read. A walk would be taken. He would sit on the porch and attempt yet another definition of himself. Lunch would be prepared. He would go into the village for groceries, come back, and throw rocks into the lake. He would collect driftwood. Firewood would be gathered and the Kalamazoo stove gotten red hot. The wind would blow papers over the porch and he would pick them up. Reading and staring at the lake. He would wish that he were a writer and would get out a legal pad of yellow paper and poise a pencil over it and throw the pencil on the floor, where it would fall through one of the broad cracks, and he would stare once again at the lake.

It was, Solon concluded, hopeless. It was not willful of him to choose to live curled like a snail in the shell of his solipsism. The concentration afforded meaning and whatever dubious value could be attributed to his past. He decided to look for driftwood and went along the shoreline through the thickening tangled growth toward the point.

Almost immediately, perhaps fifty yards beyond the outhouse, he found a blooded horse head. The wood tapered narrowly from a cauliflower ear toward a magnificently carved nostril and along the way a knothole served as a warty, wild eye. Solon hurried back to the porch with his prize, stopping only to pick up a round flat stone. He would sit on the porch and polish the head with the stone until it shone with thoroughbred pride, and he would run his hand along the once quivering flesh. It would stand quiet by his touch, impervious to fire, thunder, or gunshots. Rubbing with the grain Solon watched the wood come alive under his pressure. For hours, contentedly, he rubbed and then realized how hungry he was. It startled him to discover that it was almost midafternoon. He looked with pleasure and a little awe at the head, took it inside, put it on the table and asked it how it could have wasted so much of his time without moving a muscle. You know, Solon said, I am the master here and you're my beast of burden and if I choose I can put you to work carrying the water jar. I can buy a riding crop and beat your nostrils. I can pull an Aggie and tickle your ass. Don't think, old horse, I'll spend every day combing and currying your favor.

He stood irresolute in the cabin, wondering what to do about lunch. One could drive into town and eat at the restaurant or buy luncheon meat at the A&P. Meanwhile, Aggie and that hunk of a boy were out in the middle of the lake, munching sandwiches under the blue sky, the boat rocking a little at anchor, the lines drifting aimlessly, and perhaps Aggie would wonder what could be done most economically and profitably with the passions of a seventeen-year-old boy. Solon moved her slim arms around the sunbaked neck and mushed her breasts against the hard young chest and let her eyes go blind. He was angry with himself for having let her go, having given her her head and taken as consolation prize a Trojan horse. At least, first, they might have had lunch together.

He decided to see whether Mrs. Crown had already drunk herself to sleep or whether she could still cook him something up. Chances were against him because afternoon was the worst part of her day and she was so predictable that Aggie and he had risked it once in the tiny adjoining bedroom. As he walked down the road, his irritation mushroomed and finally became so mammoth that it changed into something else. He kept visualizing Mrs. Crown lying loose and open on her bed, an arm lying over the side with the hand limp, dead in her drunk as any piece of wood to the world. Her skin would have the qualities of a blown-up balloon, smooth if one moved lightly enough over the surface and coarse and resistant if one applied a little pressure.

His imagination proved reliable. He stood over her and contemplated her slack, full lips blowing bubbles of froth in and out. Her face in sleep, flushed, was soft as melted wax before it hardened and he felt if he touched it, it would be piercing hot. She lay on her back and her robe had fallen to her sides, exposing a corridor of body from the neck to the toes, and the skin, unlike that of her face, was smooth and unlined. He eyed her and demanded a closer, more extravagant look. He raised her left arm flung out across the bed and slid in beside her. Her other arm was folded back under her neck so that one breast was taut and the other, closer to him, flabby and old. The firm breast reminded him of a light-colored, round pumpernickel. He spread out his hand, hooked into a claw, over the breast without touching it and, a forefinger as tattooing needle, never touching the flesh, traced a fleur-de-lis over the network of blue veins, then, the finger becoming a bread knife, cut the breast into thin slices. Her eyelids, throbbing, remained closed and her mouth in sleep was busily open. He withdrew his arm and contemplated her navel. The belly button was like a kaiser roll and he again raised his hand to the duty in the air of mashing and kneading her flesh. He put his ear near her chest half expecting to hear murmurs as from a hollow shell but her heart noises, two inches away, eluded him.

Solon lifted his head and stared downward toward the luxuriant, closely woven fibers of a rich brown rug or, perhaps, the strands of a cheap wig. In any event they did not interest him and even gave him displeasure and his eyes paused at her legs, round and white and smooth except for a few bumps and smudges like the limbs of those certain trees partially shorn of bark on the point.

She twisted on her side toward him and her arm found its way around his neck. He lay still and disturbed, breathless under the weight. Her knees had come up and pressed against his side. He finally dared to look at her face. Her eyes, large, unblinking, swimming in moisture, were open and staring at him. Fully clothed he felt terribly exposed, and remembered how hungry he was. He got up and fumbled at his fly although he knew it was zippered. "I came over for lunch," he muttered and rubbed his palms on his jacket. She continued to gaze at him and he began to wonder if she were even conscious of his identity or, rather, drowned in a subliminal need. Whatever she wanted he could not give to her and what he wanted, lunch, would not be offered, clearly. "See you later," he said, and walked out. He would get his car and drive to town.

Solon ate dinner alone. He cut thick slices of kosher salami, spread them with mustard and ate them between slices of Wonder bread. The food was washed down with California red wine. He ate sometime after seven, waiting as long as his hunger would let him for Aggie to tap on his door, but she didn't come. The wind from the lake was setting up a howl and whenever he opened the door to the porch the gale caught him in the throat and he choked on his salami. The kerosene lamps flickered and shadows, punch-drunk fighters, boxed on the walls. Finally he couldn't stand the cabin any longer and went into the gathering darkness to confront the lake. Waves smacked the shore and rushed away, dripping with saliva. Solon was hungry, hungry for Aggie. He wanted her back. He wanted to nip her fragile shoulder, guzzle her neck, wanted her to lie down under the butcher knife of his need and sprinkle sand in his hair, tie his shoelaces together, he wanted her. He wanted to know that nothing had changed between them and that between them was . . . nothing. Their day apart had taught him that he had a large appetite for her and that her absence was pain but he knew all about pain already. What was unknown was whether he could forget that he had desired, however briefly, her happiness.

Out on the lake a motor throbbed and Solon followed the sound as it moved away into silence. He sat on the shore and played with pebbles, piling them over his shoes. They kept falling off, refusing to play at burial. As he sat, the ground biting at his buttocks, he felt a back leaning against his and could have cried out with his need of it. "Welcome home," he said and turned swiftly to hold her. She stood up, eluding him, laughing. He was exultant, eager for her games. He snatched at an elegant ankle but she moved away.

"Not just yet, Solon," she said. He noticed then that she was different. Instead of blue jeans she was wearing a pleated skirt, cashmere pullover sweater, and high heels that balanced her precariously on the rocks. It made her seem, against the fading backdrop of pines and lake and crudely fashioned cabin, an intricate bit of high-breasted sophistication pointing toward him from a fashion magazine. He was, he felt, at a serious disadvantage although he had seen her so dressed from time to time in New York. It bewildered him to remember that he had thrown her about as carelessly as a tackling dummy.

She moved away from him, her skirt played with by the wind, and he had a sharp image of his own clean profile showing itself to the promise of woods and water. "We're leaving for New York tomorrow," she said.

He stood up. "Tomorrow? Why? What's happened?"

She laughed. "Why must something have happened? Mother and I decided we've had enough of roughing it, that's all."

He said slowly, "How do you plan to go? If you recall, you came up in my car."

"Billy. He wants to visit New York, he's never been there, can you believe it? and he'll drive us in."

"I see. I didn't realize he was old enough to drive a car. Very convenient for everybody, isn't it?"

"Very," said Aggie. She extended her arms and spun in a swift circle. "Since it's our last night together I dressed up for you. You like?"

"Can't you wait until Sunday? It's only three more days and then we can all leave together. Has it been so impossibly tedious that you have to cut and run? I thought we were having fun and games together."

"I had much fun, Solon, honestly. You're a laugh a minute," said Aggie. "It's just that mother and I get horribly restless too long away from the city. That's all. No great master plot. Nothing devious or subtle about it so why make a fuss?"

"You go out on the lake with Billy for a day and then you take off with him for New York," said Solon, angry with himself for caring, more for showing it, for making himself as ridiculous in her eyes as she made him out to be.

Aggie laughed. "That too. That's one way of putting it. Billy's a sweet, adoring boy and it'll be fun showing him New York. He showed me one kind of fish and I'll show him another."

Solon stared savagely at the lake. In the now tricky light it was a wind tunnel empty of everything but sound and he could imagine himself fluttering like a tone-deaf bat, bruising himself against walls. "Did you catch yourself a fish, then?" he said bitterly.

"Yes of course. It was glorious. Billy took out the hooks and threw them back because they were just perch and chub and too bony and you were right. They didn't hurt at all."

"Very professional," said Solon. "You'll wow your friends in New York with your fish stories."

"I can't wait to brag," she said. She wobbled on her heels to stand beside him and laid a hand on his arm. "Dear Solon, don't be cross that we're leaving. It has been fun and I have liked being with you, but after all, we're nothing to each other that involves bitterness." She paused and then said softly, "I thought, the last night, we might play house in your cabin. Something like the girl and boy who meet on the western plains during a thunderstorm and take refuge in an abandoned hut."

Solon couldn't speak for a moment. To the end she would make of him a cardboard vagabond in a ghost town filled with vagrant chuckles. "Tell me something. Why do you think lovemaking is funny?" he said. "Why can't you treat it as something, if not respectable, at least decently serious?"

"Dear Solon," she said. "If you're in love when you make love, it's not only serious, it's eminently respectable. If you're like us, it's positively indecent to be in earnest, don't you think? It's like those military maneuvers in peacetime and what do they call those but war games? I love the way we've made love. No champagne and roses. Pinecones for the likes of us." She tugged at his arm. "Come on. Don't spoil everything with dirty talk."

He resisted her pull. "Phyllis is having a baby," he said.

She released his arm. "I know. She wrote me. I think it's wonderful for her. She'll make a grand mom."

"Wonderful, what's so wonderful about it? She despises and scorns David, now she has his child."

"I doubt that very much, very much indeed. Your reports of the death of her heart tend to be exaggerated, in my humble opinion. Anyway, the old songs take care of that: you hate the one you love."

"She doesn't love David."

"Of course she does, you silly goose."

Solon, moving quickly, caught Aggie in his arms and kissed her ungently on the mouth. She submitted passively and he let her go. "Marry me, Aggie," he said. "Let's go back to New York and get married."

She stared at him. "Just because I won't stay here three more days, because Phyl is having a baby, what?"

"I don't know. Just marry me."

She grinned, a full-lipped mirthless act. "Because you adore me and want me to be the mother of your children, what?"

"Okay then, don't marry me," he said. "Go on home with Billy. Show him the sights. Give him an eyeful."

"I will, tomorrow," she said. "Don't you want me tonight?" She leaned against him. "You're a lovely enough fellow, Solon. Not to worry."

"Sure," he said. "Lovely enough to tickle the balls off of. Goodbye, Aggie."

"Good night, Solon, and good luck."

"Same to you and your mother and fucking Billy," said Solon. He added, "I can't say it hasn't been fun."

"No," she agreed. "I couldn't say it either. Drop in when you get back to New York."

"Sure," he said. "You can show me the Bronx."

"Goodbye, Solon," she said and picked her way in the dark toward her cabin. He could imagine her tripping and falling a dozen times, battering her beautiful round knees. The hell with her knees. Billy, a hundred Billys, would kiss them and make them well.

He went to the lake's edge and trailed his hand in the water. Despite the wind, the water was not too cold. He went into the cabin and changed into swimming trunks, walked out, and then had another idea that involved going back in and getting the horse head. He carried it to the beach and bruised his bare feet on the rocks. The water was very cold against his thighs but still bearable. He pushed off, letting the horse head lead him and churned water with a scissors kicking, moving toward the center of the lake. He was mythic, a short-legged transvaluated centaur with a swollen head, its genes fouled up for good and so more historical than mythopoeic. If he came right down to it, he was an unfit companion for mermaids. Solon murmured soothing words to the head, his better half, bidding it to remain calm and not be startled by the objects hurtling around them in the unraveling waves: the flickering, rollicking lick of the waves, God, why did that hideous mockery have to pop into his mind?

He collected himself. The head and he, invincible warriors, would rescue the human damsel Aggie, tied to a floating log by villainous billy goats and set adrift without steak and champagne. Far ahead he could see with his Kryptonitic eyes her long loose hair trailing like weeds along the surface of the lake. She would be saved but only he could save her.

When his furious kick began to abate and the ache in his legs reached his brain, he realized that he had swum too far. He turned around clinging to the head in earnest, testing it for buoyancy, letting his legs drop, and fortunately the head kept him afloat. He sucked in air and realized that the water was freezing cold. It was necessary to start kicking before his legs became numb. He jerked into motion and moved tensely toward shore. His legs were heavy and listless and he had to force them through the motions. He switched to the breaststroke and found this somewhat easier. His lungs filled with anguish. Finally he felt bottom.

Solon waded in still holding the head, and the rocks played cruel games with the soles of his feet. He cried aloud with pain and, dropping the head, scrabbled in on his hands and knees. He made shore and lay on his stomach gasping.

Soon he sat up and rubbed his feet. The warmth made them throb and he cocked his head, listening to the hurt. The horse head bobbed against the shore and he went over and dragged it aground, then sat back down and continued rubbing his feet. In a few minutes, dripping and shivering, he went in and stuffed pine chunks and paper into the Kalamazoo stove. With pushing and prodding, much against the horse head's will, he managed to wedge it in with the door left open. He lit the paper and, gnawing on a piece of cheddar, lay down like a retriever in front of the fire, which, spitting and crackling, began to come at him with a lot of noise.

VII

A DAY IN THE LIFE OF A DOG

Set ye Uriah in the forefront of the hottest battle, and retire ye from him, that he may be smitten, and die.
—*II Samuel 15*

When Uriah was younger he needed no prodding in the morning. Like a child he would be at their faces, pushing with his nose until they, in sleep, would reproach him with disordered sweeps of their arms. He was better than an alarm clock and David Stein during those years was never late for his law office nor Phyllis for her classes at the university. He was pulling his weight in many ways and had much less weight to pull. It couldn't have been more than fifteen pounds, give or take an ounce.

Now he is ten. By human measurements he is seventy and that will give you some idea. Any old man with shiny scalp ringed by frail hair as he clumps toward you up the stairs will give you some idea. Uriah is ridiculous when he gallops after a blue rubber ball David bounces along the dining room rug but he still attempts the expected, and what is expected most of all is that he doesn't grow old.

Today Uriah lies curled at the foot of Phyllis's part of the Hollywood bed, buried as always under the blankets, feeling through the weight of wool the heat of the morning sun. He knows what he should do. He should crawl loose, stretch his length at one end, then the other, yawn along loosening canines, get about the business of nuzzling them awake. Instead he wriggles into an even tighter snail's shell, prepared to complain ferociously if David should so much as touch him. It's a game they've played for some time—that he's vicious—and, of course, growing old and tamer even than before (if such were possible), Uriah loves to pretend.

One wonders if he's older than he realizes, perhaps even senile. It may be that his mind is beginning to go. Memory of immediate past experience is where it's supposed to start and Uriah has forgotten that Phyllis isn't here but in the hospital. He whines in anguish. He went in the car with them because Phyllis wanted him until the last possible moment. He recalls her warm, fragrant softness as she squeezed him and mouthed his whiskers growing white. And the ride back home with David, with neither of them saying anything or looking at each other. Uriah whimpered but not as much as if he'd yet believed she wouldn't be at home waiting for him. Being of short memory he can't remember another night without her and this is why, not simply old age, he forgot her absence. The bed is endlessly long and empty, and even under the wool heated by the sun he is cold with loneliness.

David snores. No one will ever convince Uriah that David misses her the way he does or that David loves her the way he does. He stares at David unguarded in sleep, at his folds of flesh like a repulsive English bull's over his broad, flat face and rejoices that she, like himself, has a long nose with the skin drawn tightly over her cheeks.

David and Uriah use each other for play more than love. Uriah concedes he'd rather play with him than with her because, for one thing, David makes it hard for Uriah to win and, for another, Uriah can't pretend with her, he loves her too much. With David, Uriah becomes a mule and tugs at the leather strap David holds at the other end. He fastens his teeth in the strap and jerks it savagely with sideway motions until David fancies that it is time to pretend (on his part) Uriah has prevailed. Uriah becomes a wolf as David rolls him on his back and fastens square hands around his throat. Uriah rolls back his wet lips and snarls and almost breaks David's skin. He is often tempted to go all the way, and dreams of it sometimes, but never does. Uriah prefers David for games because she doesn't understand that games, to have meaning, must be won the hard way.

Phyllis dresses Uriah up from time to time and he doesn't like this at all, but, of course, he loves her. She puts sweaters on him, plastic boots, rhinestone collars. She even has a yellow neckpiece that, mindless of black hair, long nose and littleness, is supposed to make him look like a lion.

Uriah knows about love. One hears a lot of talk about it from those who don't know, or if they do, it's been only for a moment or two and then they spend their lives imitating those moments, talking about them as though they still exist. Uriah lives in love, never love past, always love present. If you love for years and stop loving for a moment, you do not love and the years are loveless. The special quality of Uriah's love is that he doesn't haggle. He is catholic in his love and divorce is a word that doesn't exist in his vocabulary.

He grows restless and hot under the lonely blanket and is not prepared to be uncomfortable simply for David now that he realizes Phyllis isn't there. A siren of terror rises in his throat and he shuts his muzzle on it. The result is a gulp of sound that would have made Phyllis laugh. He starts a sinuous crawl under the blanket toward the head of the bed and the pillow where her face should be pointing toward him and her closed eyelids ready to be licked upward, where he would pretend to suffer her smothering embrace until breath would squeeze out of him in a tight, hard grunt. Today he emerges into a world of unused linen and turns upon himself in accusatory circles of anxiety. In his childish heart, he assumes he did something bad to make her leave home. Finally he drops in a heap on the pillow, his muzzle, a triangle of gray on the whiteness, mourning toward sleeping David.

The quality of a dog's love speaks well of life because it is merciless and can continue to live. Uriah stares without mercy at David and wishes him transformed into Phyllis. He would willingly undergo the assault on his senses of the broad, fleshy form fading and reforming into the long, thin-legged beloved, and without pausing to consider whether the metamorphosis was miraculous or a product of nature or science, he would leap, jaws grinning and red wafer tongue floating, in for the love.

David, oblivious to the need for chrysalis or to Uriah's passionless stare, snored on. He would have liked to sleep, oh at least forever, because when he awakened it would be to the serious questions of birth and divided loyalties. Instead he had to awaken immediately because he had been sleeping with his right arm pinned underneath and the mass of himself had cut off the circulation at the elbow. It was an intimation of mortality, and David, not fully awake, groped for the arm. It eluded him, swinging idly as though controlled by wind and connected by a thread. He reached again and succeeded in corralling the shoulder socket. By slow movement downward he massaged his arm back to life. He awakened fully and, rubbing, stared upward, noticing again that the flat, rectangular light fixture was slightly awry. Its corners did not parallel those of the room. Whenever he noticed this, he resolved to correct it but was never in a willful enough position to do so. The morning sunlight lighting up the fixture from the top exposed shadowy figures of moths dead against the glass. David reminded them that they no longer need serve in his house of birth and his mind sprang up to sweep the fixture clean and set it straight, but his body, unclaimed and unresponsive as usual, did nothing.

He turned toward Uriah and knowing what to expect matched the dog's round, brown stare. They looked at each other along the glistening white plain of empty pillow and David once again marveled at a dog who refused to look the other way.

"What you don't know, Uriah," said David judicially, "would hurt you. You just think she's gone but it's more than that. She's gone for your replacement, chum. Your days, old dog, are numbered." David, softened by his sense of Uriah's misery, reached for the dachshund's ear and scratched the valley behind it. Uriah, refusing to bend, nevertheless opened his mouth in reflex yawns.

David got up and went to the window. Looking down from the second story at the front lawn, brown and tough in autumn, a wet, rolled county newspaper invading the privacy of the stone walk, he felt that he was in a stranger's house, that walking dazedly, a bleeding cut on his forehead, he had been taken by the hand and led to an alien bed. Later, refreshed, having eaten another man's food, he would find that he didn't even know his name. He would be started on a series of odd jobs. He would be a laborer in a U.S. highway building gang, wash dishes in a Greek or Italian restaurant, discover he was good with figures and become a check-out cashier in a National supermarket, suddenly in a fit of revivalism know how to type and become a male secretary to an Irish lawyer, one morning know the answers to legal problems that hadn't been invented yet, and with a groan he dropped his head into his old life. He was David Stein, attorney, and lived in an old wrinkled house with a brown lawn, a dachshund eyeing him severely, and a wife, Phyllis, pregnant in the hospital, making everything strange after years of childlessness.

Since it was Saturday he didn't have to go to work. It was seven-thirty, getting-up time for weekdays, yet he could crawl back luxuriously into bed and sleep through washing, shaving, dressing, breakfast, Uriah's early morning romp, the crowding on the bus ride downtown. He wouldn't because Phyllis's pregnancy was change enough for all of them, himself, Uriah, even Phyllis.

Change was so clearly what Phyllis lived for. She could never bear the idea that life might consist of a single leaf dropping upon itself until the pile was swept away in a definitive raking. He had no doubt he loved his wife, and was much less sure of her *quid pro quo*, and tried very hard to think of ways he could mutate, or at least complicate her idea of him, but whatever he did seemed to emerge, as he examined himself from her eyes, in *inarticularity,* the kind of simulated word play that kept his timid, defensive silences around Phyllis amused.

And he kept piling up his brown, tough leaf despite himself and despite her, despite his trying to show her in so many ways (that, alas, even he, the programmer, could not decipher) that given the slightest lead-in, a smile here, a pat on the shoulder there, he might be a delightful raconteur, an amusing, whimsical companion, a flashing, darting, profoundly graceful, gracefully profound intellectual, a credit to his race and to her.

Well, heaven to Betsey, or was it heavens, or was it anything at all, Phyllis would be happy at last, she would make the child into her own image and leave him be, dispose of him thoughtfully perhaps, now that he had proved to be the great stud to the queen bee. Of course, this was only his idea. Naturally, even with the baby, she couldn't, or wouldn't, inhale a full aroma of love unless she tested first to see if it were cooking properly.

Uriah would be a problem, had always been a problem, but now would have serious opposition and so must retaliate with real bite in his teeth. He would have to remove the cellophane from his sharpness. Baby was the ultimate ruler of dog even in clipped poodle areas. Early Uriah had discovered that David was only a titular monarch and had wormed against the thigh of Phyllis, separating as by an early New England bundling board, the husband and wife. Sexual play involved scraping the dog loose, enduring his phlegm-choked growls, tolerating his owlish stare from the other side of the bed. It was a middle-aged performance at an extended stag party.

David often wondered if Phyllis would have respected him more if he'd grabbed Uriah by a fat, short thigh and flung him outside the bedroom door. He had never dared because, knowing the outcome, he dreaded the open scandal of weighing Phyllis's love for her dog and for him on a balancing scale. The same old refuge of *inarticularity.*

The telephone rang and knowing it would have to be the hospital he ran to answer it. It was Aggie Crown calling from the hotel, where, in a queer for her, and thus charming, show of propriety, she had insisted upon staying rather than with him in the house. "I thought I'd come over and make breakfast for you," she said, "before we go to the hospital. What say?"

"I say great, Aggie, but it isn't at all necessary. Why don't we go to I-Hop? I'll come by for you."

"I'll get a cab and be right over," she said. "For any number of reasons, including the fact that you are still my one and only Abram." And she hung up before he could protest further. It shocked him to realize that she was still tasting their time together in New York, half a decade ago, an eternity ago, and that he was more than willing to let her.

Uriah can't wait any longer and while David is dressing, trots downstairs and pees on the blond walnut leg of a dining room chair. It is a spot he has never tried before because it is much too public, but with Phyllis absent, concealment doesn't matter. He knows that he has the upper hand over David and this negates corporeal punishment. He finishes, sniffs in distaste at his own lack of form, and gallops to the front door, barking. He wishes to go out because somewhere outside Phyllis is undoubtedly waiting.

David comes downstairs drawing his belt. He is a bear of a man and looks as though, if he discovers the pee spot, he will annihilate Uriah with one cuff of his paw. But he will neither discover the spot nor, if he should, even raise his voice.

On the walk Uriah strains against the leash. He ignores oaks, maples, pfitzer bushes, hedges, fireplugs. He is not curious about formations of paper flattened against trunks by wind but keeps his long black nose with its deviated septum high in the air sniffing for Phyllis. David at the other end of the leash permits Uriah to direct their erratic course. He will not interfere, has never interfered, with Uriah's nature. He is willing to defer to the will of the dog on the theory that the dog has a superhuman sense of purpose and that he has none. Uriah's course is dog-legged but he does keep going and that, to David, is the important thing.

They finally turn back and Uriah, on the trail of his own scent, bounds joyfully forward in a straight line toward the front door. He moves without hesitation into the house, expecting that Phyllis is here, has been hiding all the time, perhaps in the fireplace, up the chimney, behind the living room couch. He runs passionately upstairs to smell her out under the bed where, thin and fit as she was before pregnancy, she would have to be slender as dust. Since he can't find her anywhere he whines in rises and falls of infinite variation. David sits downstairs, smoking a pipe, and Uriah pokes at him with his nose. He is exasperated with David because David obviously knows where Phyllis is and won't tell him.

Again David felt dislocated. He was sitting with Aggie at his own breakfast table, on a chair as old as his marriage, and might just as well have battered through an endless storm and found, before he fell for what he knew to be the last time, a feeble light blinking through twisting branches of forest. He had kissed his wife tenderly, felt her fevered brow and promised broth from the fresh game he would kill. She was late having her first child and he was anxious about her flushed face and groans in the night when she thought he couldn't hear. If anything happened he would never forgive himself for having brought her to a godforsaken wilderness. Now, caught in a storm, lost, despairing, wondering if his wife was dying while he was wandering, he had found the isolated cabin where a strangely beautiful woman took him in, fed him, was tender, and would go back with him to nurse his wife. She had had four of her own in the forest, there was nothing to it, but he wasn't entirely reassured because this was a different brand of woman. Four of her own of *what*?

Aggie sat opposite him as they ate the bacon and eggs she had prepared. Fragmented he missed the buttered toast, golden brown, melting, prepared by Phyllis in the broiler. Aggie had made the toast in the toaster and spread butter on it afterward. A small thing that made him realize how beautiful Aggie was because he ate the unfavored toast with gratitude. While they sat he was conscious of Aggie's knees striking his own and puzzled over the physical laws that made it possible. Phyllis, longer legged than Aggie, never touched him under the table. He looked up from his eggs, and Aggie, ready, caught him with a smile. She touched his arm. "How are the eggs?"

"Fine." Actually they were too dry. Phyllis knew the secret of eggs, moistness. He was aroused. Sooner or later it had been bound to happen and sooner or later he would have been just as unprepared to be alone once again, once too often, with Aggie. Once before, only once, and it had spread its remembrance over him like the blanket of childhood tragedy. It might have been his grandmother dying and his rushing toward her dead body only to be entangled in his mother's black skirts. Just once and never again and yet it was a dress-parade part of his life that gobbled up huge swatches of the rest. It wasn't the sight of her loveliness that lingered, dark eyes or curved mouth, nor a particular fragrance of perfume or smell of pores or the taste of her wet mouth on his. The memory was of a capsule of time captured in sensation and he could see and hear and smell it although for all he knew it hadn't happened.

He could define his taste for Phyllis because it was his, built out of years of knowing. Her body was interwoven with his own the way strings of euonymus mingled with their slats of back porch. He invited the whiplash of tongue, the vitality of mind when she stabbed at him, and he could only be sad that his return offerings seemed to offend her. Between them was no erection of loving that was beyond a knowledge of love and now that she was having his child he felt that the very fact of his loving was a burden to her. She simply would have no time to carry the weight of his affection.

He mooned at Aggie's breast tight against a gray ski sweater and she, sensitive as a lie detector to passion, arched toward him. He smiled but not easily, conscious of his grossness, of her beauty, of the romances that had passed him by, of the short, tough sessions in bed with his wife that made sex a series of clothespins locked to a line, of the embryo that was reaching toward birth in an elastic womb. He had never laid his wife without love but somewhere along the way he was transformed from prince into frog, grunting and wheezing with froggish frustration. Had he failed Phyllis's vision? He didn't even know if she had one. He knew he had failed some pseudonymous busybody on the day he was born broad and round, so why not Phyllis?

David knew that Aggie desired him, perhaps truly was in love with him. He knew because Aggie was a beauty who could afford transparency. She was a beauty and David at least loved the idea of her beauty. Now that Phyllis had her pregnancy he couldn't even feel guilty about the soft and moving parts of sex offering itself. Aggie made no bones about it. Aggie loved a man's world. It could easily be the other way around. Man's world loved Aggie, and that world, loving, was hard to refuse. He reached across years of dogged fidelity, drunk on eggs and bacon, and cupped Aggie's breast in his hand. She pushed toward the palm.

"I love you, Aggie," he said. He did love her, loved the thought of

her, the thought of the princess taking the frog to bed with her knowing the frog would never metamorphose, completely modern, hating the prince, loving the frog.
"I love you too, David. I do."
"Let's go, Aggie," he said rudely. "Let's go. We've waited long enough. We published our banns years ago in New York. What have we been waiting for?"

Uriah watches soberly from the other bed, the labial corners of his mouth curled in a lemon-sucking grimace. He is sitting on his round soft rear and bracing himself on his front legs so that his muzzle sniffs them out. They move in thoughtless, self-seeking patterns behind the drawn drapes. They wander through heavy breathing, exploring mouths and hands never more gentle, catching their delight in a network of quick gasps. Uriah is strangely still. His impotent whines, probes of his wet, black nose, sharp, explosive barks are absent. It is discovered that his jealousy is as pure as his love and that he is not jealous of the act of love. He mourns for his mistress, and the intertwine of limbs would not keep him for an instant beyond Phyllis's return. He would warn the lovers if by a premonition reserved for pregnant wives Phyllis would gather her bloated body, crawl into her clothes, summon a cab and go home to protect her heart and hearth. He would fly up barking with joy and David would know that bark above all others and before Phyllis could labor upstairs he would tie the fire rope to the window frame and lower Aggie down to safety, the trench coat crawling up her legs, revealing the quick and eager thighs.

Uriah indifferently turns away at the climax and stiffens momentarily into attention at the rattling of a woodpecker outside the window. He curls on Phyllis's pillow, burrowing in for the fading scent of her hair. The irony of it as she lies relaxed and lighthearted occurs to Aggie for she says, "Really, David, that dog." She laughs aloud, it is much too absurd.

David, busy memorizing the incredible lines of breast and stomach with thick fingers, remembers that he had a moment of indecision about Uriah, whether to leave the door slightly ajar or to shut it tight, knowing that the dog's india rubber nose, through habit, would push the door open, and that Uriah would jump on the bed, not to see but to remember. David decided he wanted Phyllis's dog there because it made everything open and aboveboard and showed that David had nothing to hide. Too many excuses spoiled the broth. Uriah wouldn't hesitate to tell all. The moment he saw Phyllis he would yap his fool head off.

"I'm sorry," says David. "I forgot all about him." He is aware that he has already begun to talk differently, to phrase his difficult words into easy lies and this gives him renewed strength of purpose. He knows that change is imperative, for him, for Phyllis. It must be, he now insists, that his failures were in believing that honesty was dynamic about trivia like his family life and could effect changes. He is beginning dimly to realize that honesty lies outside of time, literally has no time for small change such as he.

He is once more aroused. How much he has wanted to be known: does this beautiful, sensual woman really know him? She is lovely, what can she know of bulky David? But she claims she does and he is tired of fighting for the truth American-style. He will dive deeply into the mainstream of her knowledge and flail about with fleshy self-satisfaction.

They took Uriah for his second walk of the day. David held the dog with a stiff straight arm on the leash and asked himself why the stiffness and straightness were familiar. Of course he had many times walked Uriah but never before with Aggie, usually with Phyllis who held the leash. Aggie's presence made the walk strange so it was something else. David looked with blind eyes at his new world. The autumn had turned mild after a cold night and the sun was shining warmly on his sinful skin. He wore a blue denim golf jacket half zipped up the front, and God help him, he felt warm all over. Beside him, bumping him as she swung his arm, his nest of love kept pace, dressed in her gray sweater and skirt and looking for all the world and his neighbors to see like a young girl who had just gotten engaged—no, less, fraternity pinned if they still did such things. He studied the oaks lining the parking. No longer attached to summer they were bare of leaves, their branches standing starkly against the sky. They refused to cotton to his budding romance but that was all right because urbanized romance had absolutely no sense of season.

Uriah's fat, circular, soft-skinned rump bobbed and David computed the pounds of love that had gone into the making of such a perfect roundness. Its texture belonged uniquely to those creatures, human or otherwise, who were kept, whose function it was to be preserved from struggle. Uriah, human, would be old-fashioned pink, female, full-breasted, endlessly arranging curls, polishing toenails, creaming her skin, preparing by day for the evening to produce her keeper, the depository of a nineteenth-century way of life that had conveniently overlooked the obligatory difficulties of twentieth-century women's manhood.

Perhaps, David thought and almost hooted aloud at the absurdity of the thought, this was where he had fallen down. Perhaps deep down Phyllis craved superficiality, yearned to be pink and soft-skinned and full-breasted, or at least to be treated as if she were, and all he had to do was cram her deeply into silken nightgowns and satin coverlets and order her to croon love songs into his neck instead of Uriah's. But if this were all true wouldn't they be vulgar liars pretending to metaphysical thrones of being and wouldn't they, inevitably, be flung out by the centrifugal force of truth?

To tell the truth he was a dismal fellow, ridiculous, rubbing a magic lamp for verities, which were simply that Aggie wore sheer garments as nakedly and purely as earth wore grass, that she surrendered as fearlessly to the weight of his manhood as a drone did to his queen. As she was a woman beyond proof, she made him so as a man, and Uriah was a liar of a dog pretending to be a ball buttered with love.

They walked along the short avenue bisecting his own longer street and the parallel one to the east. He was reminded of the borders set in rubber floor tiles, the long strips spelling those in between, and he felt, as they turned the corner and moved on, as if he were in a gigantic room and each square of sidewalk were plastic to his touch. The street parallel to his own was newly supplied with houses distinguishable from one another, in the contemporary manner, with gimcrackery that only made them look more depressingly alike. Here and there were bits of bushes and vines struggling to grow, oak and redbud saplings, and stolid black gaslight posts. Usually the street, its newness, demoralized him but now he felt as though he belonged. Aggie and he would move into one of the beautiful shells, unlined, uncracked, faceless and odorless except for the sweet smell of insecticide, the floors smoothly seamed against the walls—they could easily leave everything he knew and loved behind. A perfect anomie. No clouts of ivy roots to ram like a wrecker's ball against *these* stone foundations. As safe from seepage as any mausoleum. The cellar was where they would live, in the recreation room, safe from tornadoes.

They don't know me here, thought David. One block from my house and they don't know me. I'm a stranger in my own home town walking a hot dog with an exotic foreign lady, and if they wonder at all they wonder how I, a garden-variety toad, could have corralled such a woman.

They turned the corner and walked the short leg back to his block in silence. Uriah, on familiar ground, quickened his pace, or, rather, stopped jerking toward various trees and headed for home. Just the sight of the older houses, varied in size and shape, bewildered David and he wondered if the familiar would ever again be recognizable for what it had been. Just now he was walking along the worn round cobblestones of a Balkan town buried in the mountains, and framed in a window of each tilted house was a face he had once known, long ago before he'd set out for America to make his fortune. And here he was back, with a made-to-order American wife, a beauty to make the head spin, a queen such as the village, with its black teeth and twisted legs and bent noses, had never seen. Soon they would emerge, a few of the bolder at first, then the rest, and they would inquire timidly, "David, David Stein, it is you?"

"Yes, it is I, David Stein, and this is Aggie, my beauteous American wife."

And they would nod and look shyly at each other, and finally a great shout would go up, and in the evening they would dance, arms linked, at the great hall in their native costumes to do him honor. They would deck Aggie out, oh-and-ah over the silken texture of skin. "Ah, David Stein, David Stein, ah. Always you were the very devil of a frog."

Tired, he quickened the pace. He wanted to get home and sit in his chair, the soiled one in the living room. Perhaps, somehow, it had not yet wandered to a new place.

They are three houses away from home when Cyrus, the German shepherd, moving silently as always, comes from his own backyard and pads toward them. He is the old warrior with scars buried in his fur that David has always liked for the way his pointed ears stand, even in age, ready for life, ready for death. He is king of the block's domesticated animals and has never stood for nonsense; he has fought the good fight and now, too old really to win, is respected and left alone by the dogs who might beat him. Cyrus has never more than sniffed at Uriah, small, plump, baby-toothed old man of a dog, and Uriah, short legs braced and short hair rising in a ruffle on his back, has never provoked him. David knows all this, knows he has passed with Uriah in safety for years, and yet this time his hand grows clammy on the leash. He is conscious of terror, and jerks involuntarily on the leash just as Cyrus reaches toward Uriah for his usual sniff. Uriah is jerked upward slightly by the pull and, off-balance, terribly aware of Cyrus and what he might be, becomes frightened. He swings away from Cyrus in a swift, ambiguous spasm and Cyrus, old warrior, as automatically as if he were a western gunman drawn upon from the shadows, bares his teeth in a noiseless snarl and sinks them deeply into the circle of Uriah's rump. Uriah squeals, a long, shrill agonizing note, and thrashes desperately at the end of the leash to get away, but David, frozen, has gripped the other end with an iron will, not his, someone else's, someone's. And then he had it: the blind man long ago on the morning bus. When the man got off downtown, his arm was locked so into his dog, Corky. The blind leading the blind in an eternal roundelay.

Aggie, too, is motionless after having brought up a hand to cover her mouth. The two humans stand by, and Cyrus, forgetting why he attacked Uriah, prepares to finish him off for sure and will certainly do so, but his owner suddenly appears with a garden rake and strikes him across the side. Cyrus merely grunts—he will never squeal—and trots away. Uriah squirms and screams.

David picks up the keening dog, blood oozing from the rump, and runs awkwardly for his car parked in the driveway.

"Wait, David, I'm coming with you," says Aggie running after him.

"No. Please. I can handle it. Please. Go home, Aggie. I can handle it. I'll call you."

David puts the car in reverse. The grinding of the gears cuts atonally through Uriah's yelps. He backs out of the driveway. As he starts forward it seems that he will never escape Aggie and his neighbor standing at the curb, murmuring to each other, the man's eyes busy with Aggie's breasts.

David, in rage, balls aching, pulls and beats his flesh, with a fist pounds at it, as if by sufficient hammering on himself, he can put Uriah out of his misery.

VIII

THE DAY OF TRIALS

— I do not choose to run.
One of our presidents said that and to show the quality of my mind I don't remember who it was. I, Solon Pepper, with an excellent memory, don't bother to remember most names, including those of witnesses in trials I, a trial lawyer with considerable skill, conduct. Waller, my friend from Harvard Law days with whom I choose to share an apartment, says it's because I play too hard at being aristocratic. His statement, meant to annoy, pleases me. Patronization of trivial people is what makes a champion. It permits him to concentrate his energies on the main chance. I have had Aggie Crown for three whole months while Waller is half-crazy with frustration. The president's remark. It shows the quality of *his* mind: spare, firm. Impressive. A lean mixture of will and rectitude. Calvinistic, and I remember. Hardly memorable to the college student I defend for murder in the second degree but with a memorable phrase to his credit. One Aaron Farrelly likes to use: I do not choose to fight in an imperialistic war. I do not choose to listen or be polite to my elders. I do not choose to consider law of the slightest importance. I do not choose.

I hold Farrelly in contempt but not for the reasons you might think. Not even for his indifference to the law. I hate his corrupt idea of nobility. Farrelly was tried for murder because he defended his wife, which is hardly noble. He's a muddy thinker attacking a social institution by defending another.

I run all of the time. I am running now, stride for stride, with Waller, who also chooses to run. It keeps us spare, lean, hard-bellied—our choice. More important, it tests our right to Aggie sitting on the grass beside the cinder track. She waits for the winner which is as it should be.

Farrelly is wrong. His crowd occupies police stations like they used to, long ago in the sixties. Community sing. Follow the dancing ball. I go it alone, in the courtroom, in my jousts with Waller, and for no silly abstractions like justice or truth or morality. I do it for Aggie. Waller does it for Aggie. For her we will fight, asking for and giving no quarter. Farrelly is soft and heroism is merciless.

I correctly judge Waller's temper. He was too anxious and started the two-mile run at too fast a pace. I lag behind for the first mile, pull abreast at a mile and a half and am ready to make my move. I push ahead of the whistle in his lungs and cross the finish line a good twenty yards ahead. It was certain that Aggie would be mine for another week since I do not lose in push-ups, the next test, and all I need is two out of three. We won't even get to arm wrestling. I trotted over to Aggie and got my fine, hard kiss on the mouth. Waller nods, grim in defeat. He is in a terrible mood after three months of abstinence. I cupped my hand around Aggie's familiar breast before I stood up and Waller has to look because that is the rule. Neither of us dreams of breaking our rules. Farrelly must learn there was no honor without rules.

We shower together in our apartment, another rule. As the winner of the race, I am privileged to soap Aggie's body. I lingered at her breasts and belly and buttocks and Waller must watch.

Afterward, nude, we go into the living room and begin the push-ups. On the day of trials, Sunday, we remain naked in the apartment until the next morning. We were permitted to hide nothing from each other, not even the ache of the loser. One of our responsibilities was to face defeat openly. We don't need to count push-ups. The last man up won. My mind is free to refresh the memory of my special victory that leads to three months of Aggie. The winner of the lost cause got three months, and in our year together only I won a lost cause. I disprize what Farrelly stands for but he is the instrument of my greatest triumph. And when I beat Waller at push-ups, I keep Aggie for another week.

—I want to make it perfectly clear so that we understand each other. I cannot condone what you did or the circumstances that led you to be there. To be brutally frank, I cannot say that I find you particularly palatable. Having told you this, I want you to know that I will defend you to the best of my ability. I can promise you that.

I say this to the long-haired, foul-fleshed, outdated boy. He looked at me with his self-communing grin and said—Peace, man.

—I hope you will be as frank with me as I am with you. You will have no reason to regret it. I will never betray your trust. Whatever you say will be held in the strictest confidence. You killed a police officer and they throw the book at you. In all modesty you have one chance—me.

—The good book?

—Please pay attention. They crack you like an egg. I can't sufficiently emphasize the gravity of your situation. If you were ever serious in your life it should be now. When and if I am successful in rescuing you from the brink of disaster where your folly has placed you, perhaps we, you and I, may have some laughs together. I can have a good time as well as the next guy, provided it's the right time. Meanwhile you must help me to help yourself.

—But don't you think that God as well as you may be on my side? Do you think a little prayer, to God, and you, too, of course, might help?

—Smart-assism won't help you a bit. Take my word for it.

—What can I say?

—Say anything. Start anywhere. In your own words tell me what happened. You may think you know it all but you don't know anything about law. I know everything. I am the judge of what's important.

—Yes, I think you are. I'll start at the beginning. I have a hunch you'd like that.

I know he thinks I am a fool, and he knows I know he is a fool and I waited impassively. I want him to be completely sure he knows what I know.

—My father is president of a nuts and bolts company. My mother is a graduate of Bryn Mawr.

I look at him. I know the value of uncompromising eyes. Hard as steel. Hard as my muscles. I look at his scraggly beard, his hair to his shoulders like a watered-down Sir Lancelot, his brown eyes soft and sticky as semen.

—I am acquainted with your father and admire him very much. But, unfortunately Freud and his aphorisms are no defense in a court of law. Not for cop killing.

And he laughs, flashing beautiful white teeth that look out of place in his tangled beard. I was pleased to have him know I could be as smart-ass as he.

—Iodine 131 constitutes a specific fraction of the total fission produce. If iodine 131 is in the grass, and the grass is in the cow, and the milk is in the child, is it 175 or 1,200 rads of radiation? What matter of degree is it?

—Murder in the first degree could mean death. Capital punishment is back in style, you may have heard. Murder in the second degree could mean imprisonment from ten years to life. They see you coming. They stick things in your rear end you can't dream of. What have you told the police?

—Both hard and soft detergents are clearly toxic to goldfish and mosquito fish, which indicates a similar toxicity to other fish that are omnivorous like the goldfish—carp, suckers, catfish, et cetera—and carnivorous like the mosquito fish—bass, trout, et cetera.

—Have I said that I am a very patient man? I am, let me assure you. I have my own reasons for defending you. Sooner or later I think you'll realize you're not on a fishing trip. They carve guys like you up for breakfast. They feed you to the carp and trout. If you're trying to annoy me into dropping the case, be advised it won't work. I have too much respect for your father and mother and for myself to do that. Sooner or later you'll get awfully worried about what's going to happen to you. Whether you like it or not, you're no different from anybody else. You won't enjoy being screwed by your cellblock chums. I can wait. Go ahead. You talk and I'll listen. I have reasons of my own.

—You keep saying that and it's very impressive. May I inquire as to your reasons of your own? My father's money?

—No, and my reasons are of no concern of yours. I'm sure they would only bore you.

—I assure you they wouldn't but that's neither here nor there, is it? All right, then. To begin at the beginning, which is where it all started, the question before us is one of survival.

—I couldn't have phrased it better myself. Bearing that in mind, did you confess to the police?

—I'm afraid I did. I confessed that the normal cleansing mechanism of the lung is interfered with by irritant gases from industrial wastes, cigarette smoke, automobile exhausts and coal fumes so that the bronchial passages are narrowed and the mucus blanket thickened, that each of us to survive still needs his twelve to fifteen thousand daily liters of filtered air, and that is getting harder and harder to come by.

—I hope you told them that. Did you also tell them why you killed the cop?

—I like to think so, but they wouldn't listen. They weren't interested in anything I said. It's a problem of communication.

I stood up.

—I see what you mean. I certainly do. I have to leave, but don't worry, I'll be back. I find your conversation very stimulating and I'm ready to listen at any time. I think I mentioned that you are in serious trouble and that you are lucky to have a patient man defending you. Whether or not you care to lift a finger, I intend to leave no stone unturned. I intend you to be found not guilty even though you confess that the moon is made of purple cheese or that Betelgeuse did it. Meanwhile, say whatever you like to the police. That isn't my usual advice but why should I be selfish? They might as well profit along with me in your cogent and penetrating views on matters of life and death—your life, your death.

—I appreciate your interest, he says. I really do.

—Just remember I have reasons of my own as well as a few profundities like, shave off your beard. Clean-shaven is in. Trim your hair. Crew cuts are in. Take a bath. Run a mile, do push-ups. Aerobics are in. You might also wish to consider a few of the deeper and more sinister implications of the jury system.

—I'll certainly take your suggestions under advisement. But, I must confess, only for reasons of my own.

—Do. I'll appreciate it. In the meantime, I'll talk to your wife. If she's anything like you, I'm sure it will be an entertaining experience. I would hope she doesn't want a broom handle stuck up your behind.

—I am humbly grateful to have you defend me despite my long hair and all. Give my wife my love.

I look at him, I think of Aggie and I say—You don't know the meaning of the word.

He gave me that hairy-assed smile and suddenly, to believe it I had to be there, his eyes filled with tears. These wimps. These unholy, bloodless wimps.

I confess that my arms were getting tired. I watch Waller from the corner of my eye. He gave no sign of weakening. His body is stiff as a bar of steel, according to the rule, and he has never before lasted this long. Aggie, out of my range of vision, was silent. None of us speaks until the trials are over and the victor reaps his reward. This is the rule. Waller and I knew the value of silence. It stood a lawyer in good stead and it exemplifies our manliness. Waller never won at push-ups but he seems to be inspired. If he makes it in push-ups it was a standoff and everything depends on arm wrestling which is anybody's guess. Arm wrestling is the unpredictable one. Either of us may win. Ignoble thoughts assail me: perhaps I grow soft with success. Three months open, exclusive, notorious possession of Aggie weakens my moral fiber. Three months was not ideal. Or I waste time rehashing my triumph with Farrelly. I dissipated my powers of concentration. My arms twitch like severed worms and I must not lose my head. I needed my muscles for arm wrestling. I must begin to concentrate on that, save myself for that. I eased to the floor and lay there with my face buried in the rug. I lose the push-ups. I heard the sharp drawing of breath behind me and frown because Aggie violated the rule. I store up the memory of this. Aggie must be chastised. She knew that as well as we do.

Waller and I stand up and I nod in defeat which is the rule. I like to think that my face is as grim as his. Our hawks' eyes search each other for hints of weakness. I find none in his nor he in mine. I was strong again. I concentrated all my energies on arm wrestling. I allow no other thought to contaminate my mind. This is my edge. Waller was desperate to win. He *must* win and I only want to with all of my heart.

We settled into place at the table. Aggie sits nearby in my field of vision. I shake my head and frown. She violated another rule and she jumps and moves away. I erase the irritation from my mind. Waller and I touch, grasp hands. We lock into place and the pressure begins. Immediately he is rash and I know I will win. He realizes his mistake and lets up too late. We both knew I am now stronger than he. I looked into his eyes and saw the fatal traces of doubt. We notice together that Waller's arm was bent a fraction. It is the beginning of the end. I saw no reason to delay and began his downward movement. It was over. Aggie was mine for another week.

Waller stares at his vanquished arm on the table and I wait. He said nothing and I began to get angry at the violation of the rule. Finally he mumbles—I am your servant to do with as you will.

—Thank you, I say, not without annoyance.

He was in bad shape to play with the rules. And Aggie's transgressions leave something to be desired. She sat leaning forward, breasts pointing downward as if she had nothing better to do. But finally she says as she must—Solon has proved his love and has won my heart. Let him fuck me.

I do not hide my displeasure at her tardiness. We went into the bedroom and I climb into bed with Aggie while Waller watches as is the rule. I notice that Aggie lies limp as she had been known to do before. I decided to punish her infractions and thought of other things to avoid an erection. She lay there and Waller watched. Patience is always my ally.

Wanda Farrelly was even more beautiful than Aggie. I can't believe my eyes. She was graceful and fragile with the bones of a bird. She is dressed in a humble cotton garment. Her blonde hair of the finest silk falls below her delicate shoulders and I think of the dirty, scratchy body of Farrelly crushing her with his corrupt weight. It was another instance of marriage yoking beasts with beauties. I am proud of my lean, hard, immaculate body and I beg her indulgence while I remove my jacket and arrange it carefully on a chair. She looked at my muscular torso and I am thankful she has a moment with a real man. I informed her that I would defend her husband to the best of my ability. I do not tell her that she will be better off if he goes to jail. I do not tell her that I defend him for reasons of my own. When I put my pen to legal pad, she tells me her story.

—Aaron has kept the faith. He is an Indian scout with all the Indians on scrabble reservations. He is a knight in an age of dark horses. In more ancient times he would be on the steering committee of the Student Non-Violent Coordinating Committee. He would be a leader of Students for a Democratic Society. He would be gorgeously active in CORE and ACTION and W. E. B. Du Bois. He would have marched on Washington and Selma.

—He would have been a mighty busy boy. He's been busy enough, hasn't he? to land face down in the muck. And you?

—I am his wife, she said and I nodded with a sympathetic ripple of my jaw muscles.

—We gathered at the police station lobby to protest the arrest of some of our group. They were demonstrating at the hotel where the president was giving his speech on aid to the Contras. I brought a thirty-cup silver coffee urn and plugged the cord into the lobby electric outlet. There were thirty of us sitting on the lobby floor. Six uniformed policemen were there and two superior officers, one a Captain Brimm who addressed us informing us he was a police officer and that we were creating a security problem. That we were interfering with the normal business of the police department by blocking the normal flow of traffic. He ordered us to disperse and vacate the lobby. If we failed to comply with his order, we would be arrested on charges of public peace disturbance and interfering with a police officer. He repeated the statement twice more but we did not move. The policemen formed a line near the elevators at the rear of the lobby and advanced toward us to make us leave the building through the front doors. Captain Brimm told us we were under arrest and to get up and walk to the booking desk. We did not move. They began picking us up and carrying us out to the detention cell. Aaron and I were the last ones left. A policeman, Bradley Barrett, pulled me up with one hand. In his other he held his nightstick which he raised above his head. I don't know why he did this. Aaron broke loose from the two policemen hauling him out, grabbed Bradley Barrett's nightstick and struck him on the back of the neck. Bradley Barrett fell to the floor with a broken neck and died. That is how it happened. A policeman hit Aaron between the eyes with his fist and Aaron fell down. That is the story.

—Very well narrated. Very succinct. I have it all down, I say, flexing my fingers. Here is how it is. Your husband's situation is extremely grave. For reasons of my own I will do whatever I can to save him. Will you do the same?

She looks at me with eyes fully open to the light.—Yes. Anything.

I admire her devotion. She was a worthy object of adoration if I was not already committed.

—Good. You must take the stand and tell your story. You must brace yourself for the ordeal.

—Of course, she says. I will do anything I can. I will die if it will help.

I am impressed by her devotion to such a loathsome creature and I wish to show her she might have someone better, someone worthy of fidelity. I threw my shoulders back and expanded my chest.

—The killing of an officer of the law attempting to make a lawful arrest ordinarily cannot be justified as self-defense. *State v. Bronson.* Though homicide was committed in resisting the illegal arrest of accused's son, if it was committed with express malice, it sustained a conviction of second-degree murder. However, the statutes provide that homicide is justifiable in the lawful defense of a wife when there shall be reasonable cause to apprehend immediate danger of some great personal injury to her. Your husband, we must admit, killed a cop perhaps overzealous in the doing of his duty. Nobody likes a cop killer.

Nobody likes a cop killer's wife. This is a certified, bona fide lost cause, no sense pulling punches, but for reasons of my own I intend to prevail. It's in my lap and it's all up to me. I must choose the right jury, I must make the right argument and it won't be easy. Nobody can say it will be easy. I'll need all the help I can get and a little more.

—I will do anything to save Aaron, said Wanda. *Anything.*

Aggie gets restive. She examines my male organ. She pummeled it, kissed it. I allowed her to make amends for her sins of omission. Waller looks away which is not permitted. I tired of the sport and finished off the exercise in a quick, explosive burst. Aggie lay beneath me with her eyes closed. I stand up and confront them.

—Aggie Crown. You drew a deep breath when I lost the push-ups. You sat in my field of vision during arm wrestling. When I won, you delayed in honoring me. John Waller. You delayed in certifying my victory. You looked away during sexual intercourse.

They are silent. They must do penance. It is the rule.

—Solon, said Aggie. It's all over with us. John and I are in love. We want to get married. I'm sincerely sorry that we've failed to live up to the rules. I wish there were some way to make amends, some words that would make it easier.

I waited for Waller and he nodded. —You won and earned a week. We can't let you have it. We let you have Aggie once more for old times' sake and you must realize how painful it was for two people in love. You must realize how painful it is to break our vows. I'm sorry but that's the way it is.

My selection of the jury is what did it. I selected conservatives, homeowners, Chamber of Commerce, American Legion. I choose the believers in the law, defenders of the faith. I struck the bedeviled bleeders and question-begging liberals. My jury found the defendant not guilty. Justifiable homicide in the killing of a man in blue. They bent over backward to be fair. They would not use their emotions to sway the law. I pay them with my respect.

Farrelly is another story. The foreman says he is not guilty but I know he is and he knows that I know. He looks at me with his soup-stained smile and attempts to hide behind a thanks-but-no-thanks. My unyielding glance forced his graceless gratitude behind his beard and, lifting my chest, I stand clear of him and accept the token of Wanda's weeping. He knows the victory was mine, not his, and that it will be ever so.

I don't mind in the least what Waller and Aggie have decided to do. I am very sorry for them and they know I am because they can't look at me. To be perfectly truthful, I was relieved. Three months with Aggie is an awfully long time and not once do I break the rules.

—I wish you all the luck in the world. You have my blessings, you really do. You two keep the apartment, of course. I imagine you have a lot to talk about.

And I leave without another word. I dress and left them to the codeless, clamorous language of love.

IX

A DAY IN THE LIFE OF GOD

I go to Phyllis and David. It is as they say, a fine spring day, fragrant with cut grass, giant peonies yellow at the center, and climbing red roses. I wander in their garden in the cool of the afternoon while they sit on the back porch with their dachshund, Uriah, and Phyllis's bachelor younger brother, Solon.

Phyllis is a killer. She once spared a squirrel. She once lost her baby. I know I am not being fair but whoever said I was fair? She has destroyed mosquitoes, flies, spiders, water bugs. Beyond that, urban, she won't go. Mice crawl her pantry while squirrels bowl in her attic. She dislikes me for having made the "modern" leap, for having set up jury boxes of elders, gray-snouted and silver-whiskered.

While I walk in the garden in the cool of the day, Phyllis points to the yard. "Look," she says, "a rabbit." The creature pauses before his white ball bounces into the bushes. "Of course," she says. "Rabbits, squirrels, mice, we have them all."

"And a lion," she adds. "We mustn't forget the lion." She has sewn a neckpiece of yellow silk and taught the dachshund to dance to carnival music.

Solon has forgotten how to laugh. He beats a drum for its echoes in deaths of the heart. He fancies that he is something like me. He is nothing like me. His idea of heaven is Death to me.

David pets the lion because he wants to please his wife. He is a large, square bear, the gentle kind that dances in the circus ring.

People say that I am hard on them. What they object to is my insight. I see them think. Sometimes they beg for my conclusion.

Twilight is coming on. The cool of the dusk is Emil's trigger. This little boy next door sucks life. As we watch, he tramples honeysuckle bushes and shoots off his air rifle. He lets out a whoop. Emil is ten years old and ties cans to Uriah's tail.

Emil, grinning, holds up the rabbit. "He's been eating our tulips," he says. David hits the boy in the mouth, knocking him down. The rabbit sails as the boy screams, and the group on the porch sits. Emil holds his mouth while David retrieves the rabbit. Emil will not go without his rabbit. He shapes screams into words. "My daddy'll kill you. Gimme my rabbit."

"Go fuck yourself," says David.

The boy, coughing blood and spit, bolts for home. A bed of irises dies on the way. David buries the rabbit at the back of the yard.

Phyllis marvels at her bear. For years he has ridden his unicycle on the rim of her wedding band. She retreats to the bathroom. As she sits she dreams of a better life. They will do nothing differently yet nothing will be the same. They will whisper sweet paradoxes. A tribal David claims her with a hundred foreskins.

She peeps through latticed fingers. A mouse crouches in the corner under the sink. His whiskers twitch in an agony of mea culpa. A scream swells in her throat and she bites her tongue. Rising, she shuts the toilet lid and stands on it.

David waits for Mr. Eckart, about whom he knows very little. Mr. Eckart has a heart condition and has, all his life, objected to physical violence. His son and wife bully him. Mr. Eckart prays to me from time to time. As he goes toward David, he prays for a miracle that will save him.

I have performed in my lifetimes only one miracle and that is in effect an accommodation with Death. His consenting to my existence was a gracious act. In obedience to eternal habit, He kills me off from time to time because I never raise a finger to help him but cannot stand the vacuum: I, too, have become a habit.

Since David and Mr. Eckart, and Phyllis and the mouse, are about to engage in hand-to-hand combat, I should like to add a word about battlefield miracles. These miracles involve, of course, life snatched from Death. A silly notion that He might have to rely upon physical hinges. Or that I could snatch anything from Him:

> You attack me with sword and spear and javelin, but I attack you in the name of the Lord of hosts, the God of the armies of Israel, which you have insulted this day. The Eternal will deliver you into my hands, and I will cut

off your head and give your corpse to the birds of the air and the wild beasts of the earth.

While Phyllis stands on her toilet lid, Mr. Eckart says to David, "Pick on somebody your size. I'm here to beat the shit out of you." His eyes plead with David to understand. Emil smacks his swollen lips over the cleansing of David's bowels.

A shaggy dog, David wags his tail. His body seeks a universal gesture. Naturally, as a man he has become equivocal. He smiles. It is a grimace. He extends his hand, palm upward. It closes into a fist.

Mr. Eckart, powered by unfought battles, lashes out. It is a cunning attack. He kicks David in the balls and David, wrestling with the idea of justice as fairness, writhes on the grass. Emil, radiant, digs up the rabbit. Mr. Eckart prays he can escape before he coughs up the victory.

Solon watches from the porch. He laughs a forgotten laugh that he never knew, through clenched teeth. When David returns to the porch, they sit and search for words. I, in the cool of the evening, have their words. It is a case of mistaken identity:

> Here is God wearing me out, dazing me. My gauntness proves my guilt, it is an open evidence against me. He flings me down and rends me in his rage, he shows his teeth at me. When I was happy, he, he crushed me, he caught me by the neck and mangled me. He set me up to be his target, his arrows rain upon me, piercing my vitals without pity, till my entrails ooze out on earth.

Upstairs, Phyllis moves from the toilet seat toward the door. The mouse is a genuinely miserable mouse. Phyllis escapes to the porch. She entertains the thought that something bad has happened. Her voice shatters the silence. "David, there's a mouse in the bathroom. I'm sick of it."

David's face is smoothed out. "Well then," she says. "What the hell?"

"He'll be gone by now," said David.

"Don't bet on it. I shut the door on him."

"What am I supposed to do?"

"Pretend he's a ten-year-old boy." She rushes to the front hall and returns with David's wooden walking stick. David rests the stick on his knees. "I'll open the door and let him out. He'll know what to do."

"Balls. Do that and I'll never forgive you. Never."

Solon grabs the stick. "Allow me," he says and goes up the stairs. He kills the mouse with the detachment of a professional assassin. Solon carries the mouse to the back porch and holds it aloft by the tail. Phyllis, hand to mouth, rushes back toward the toilet. David takes the mouse from Solon and buries the carcass in the opened grave. When he returns, Solon goes but Phyllis stays and has already forgotten she will never forgive David.

In the dying of the twilight, the German shepherd, Cyrus, growing old around the muzzle, stalks on stiff legs through the yard looking for his friend, Uriah, whom he has once, long ago, bitten in the ass. They find each other and ceremoniously sniff each other's parts. Uriah lifts his leg at a pfitzer bush and Cyrus politely does the same. Uriah, for old times' sake, pretends he is a puppy. He makes false leaps and worries Cyrus's paws. Cyrus is not too old to join in the game. He growls softly.

And I? Turning my face toward the rising astronautic moon (as they say), going more and more toward it, I continue my walk in the cool of the night.